Confidence Woman

Also by Judith Van Gieson
in Large Print:

The Stolen Blue
Vanishing Point

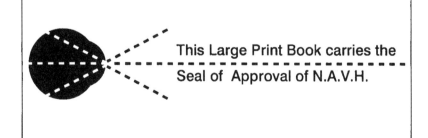

This Large Print Book carries the
Seal of Approval of N.A.V.H.

Confidence Woman

A CLAIRE REYNIER MYSTERY

Judith Van Gieson

Thorndike Press • Waterville, Maine

Published in 2002 by arrangement with NAL Signet, a division of Penguin Putnam Inc.

Thorndike Press Large Print Senior Lifestyles Series.

The tree indicium is a trademark of Thorndike Press.

The text of this Large Print edition is unabridged.
Other aspects of the book may vary from the original edition.

Set in 16 pt. Plantin by Al Chase.

Printed in the United States on permanent paper.

Library of Congress Cataloging-in-Publication Data
Van Gieson, Judith, 1941–
    Confidence woman : a Claire Reynier mystery / Judith Van Gieson.
        p. cm.
    ISBN 0-7862-4217-5 (lg. print : hc : alk. paper)
    1. Reynier, Claire (Fictitious character) — Fiction.
2. Credit card fraud — Fiction.   3. Women archivists —
Fiction.   4. Large type books.   I. Title.
PS3572.A42224 C66 2002b
813'.54—dc21   2002022880

This book is dedicated to
Amanda Howard, who is going to be
a very confident woman.

Thanks to Dominick Abel,
Linda Howell,
and Charles E. Wood
for their always valuable advice and support.

Chapter One

The fear of anyone who lives alone is to die alone and not be missed or discovered until the body begins to smell. Claire Reynier didn't live alone until she was fifty. By then her children were grown and she was divorced. She had a rewarding job, she remained connected to family and friends, but it only took one night in her new house in the Albuquerque foothills to know the fear of dying alone. She was aware that in a sense everyone dies alone, but most people die believing they'll be missed.

When she heard that Evelyn Martin died alone in her house, that no one reported her missing and that it was weeks before her body was found, Claire's rational side said that once someone was dead, the circumstances of the death weren't important. Her heart responded that to die unnoticed meant a life had had no meaning.

She learned about Evelyn from Detective Dante Amaral, who called at eight-thirty one morning while Claire was finishing her tai chi exercises, settling into the infinite ultimate stance, imagining she was balancing empty spheres between her hands and her knees. When the phone rang, her first thought was that nature abhors a vacuum and that one effect of turning one's mind into an empty bowl was that something comes along to fill it up.

Detective Amaral's voice had a soft, dreamy quality as if he hadn't quite woken up himself. "Is this Claire Reynier?" he asked.

"Yes." She sat down on the sofa with the phone in her hand, glanced out the window and saw that the Sandia Mountains were gray as a dove in the morning light.

"My name is Detective Dante Amaral. I am with the Santa Fe Police Department."

Why on earth would a Santa Fe detective be calling her? Claire wondered. Her first thought was for the safety of her children, though neither of them was anywhere near Santa Fe.

"Are you acquainted with a woman named Evelyn Martin?" Detective Amaral asked.

"Evelyn? We went to school together years ago. I've seen her a few times since."

"Yesterday we found her dead in her house on Tano Road. The postman noticed that the mail hadn't been picked up for some time and there was a smell coming from the house, so he called us."

"Oh, no. What killed her?"

"The cause of death has not been established yet. We found credit cards with your name on them in the house and were able to locate you in Albuquerque through Visa. Have you ever been the victim of credit card fraud, Ms. Reynier?"

"Yes," Claire admitted, "I have."

"I would like to talk to you about it and about the death of Evelyn Martin. Would you be willing to come to Santa Fe?"

He paused between words as if each was a pearl to be smoothed and polished before it left his mouth. The last sentence had the inflection of a question, but Claire understood it to be a summons. She agreed and they set a time for later in the week.

She hung up and sat still for several minutes, absorbing all she had learned. Then she began to pace from one end of her house to the other, wearing a track through her gray carpet. Her cat, Nemesis, tried to insinuate himself between her legs, but she shooed him away.

She thought back to the time the previous year when she had been the victim of credit card fraud. It began with a package that came to her house containing a silky black Victoria's Secret nightgown with deep cleavage and spaghetti straps crisscrossing the back. She knew of no one who would send her a revealing nightgown and was sure it was a mistake, although the package was clearly addressed to her and the nightgown was her size — ten. She called the store and discovered that someone had taken out credit in her name. To do so, the impersonator needed her social security number, the clerk told her, a photo I.D. (which was easy enough to fake), and a good credit rating. Claire's was impeccable.

She called the Albuquerque police and learned from a policewoman named Susan Deutsch that the crime was known as true name fraud.

"It's likely just the tip of the iceberg," Officer Deutsch warned. "You should check your credit rating with a national credit bureau to find out what else has been charged."

Claire did and was appalled to learn that the identity thief had recently opened several accounts in her name. It was too soon for the bills to arrive but the thief had already taken cash advances in the amount of $25,000 and charged another $20,000 worth of merchandise, things that Claire would never have bought for herself, including negligees and underwear from Victoria's Secret, a state-of-the-art stereo system and a TV the size of a window. The merchandise purchased with her good credit was so uncharacteristic of Claire that she'd had the sensation an evil twin was sending her a malignant message. She was able to establish that the thief had used preapproved credit card offerings that had been mailed to her house. Officer Deutsch said that the credit offers could have been stolen from her mailbox or by what was known as Dumpster diving, rifling through her trash.

"You didn't tear up those offerings before you threw them away?" the policewoman asked.

"No," Claire admitted.

"You should have."

"From now on I will," Claire replied. "To open these accounts the thief needed my social security number."

"That can be obtained easily enough over the Internet. Your social security number also appears on various documents — bank statements, mortgage statements, mutual funds, for example."

"I never noticed that any of them were missing." Claire was meticulous about her bookkeeping.

"The perp could have taken the number from a statement and put it back in your mailbox, or the perp could have gained access to your house. Were you robbed? Did you ever entertain anyone in your house you didn't know well?"

"No."

"Have you had any untrustworthy houseguests?"

"No." Claire couldn't imagine having a houseguest who would steal from her, but after she got off the phone she looked through her calendar to remind herself exactly who had visited. There were her children, of course. She wouldn't even contemplate that they would steal from her. Her brother or her old friend Madelyn from Tucson? The bookseller friends, John Harlan and Anthony Barbour? Never. She flipped back through the pages of the calendar until she came across the name of Evelyn Martin eight months before the theft. The timing seemed off. Any credit card offers that were in the house when Evelyn visited would have expired by the time the charges took place. Eventually Claire dismissed her, too, as a possible culprit, although she considered her far longer than her other guests.

She and Evelyn had lived in the same residence at the University of Arizona in the sixties. In fact, they had been sorority sisters.

These days Claire didn't like to admit — even to herself — that she had been in a sorority, but she supposed she would have to pass that detail on to Detective Amaral. She and Evelyn hadn't been close. After graduation she saw her occasionally at reunions. Then one day Evelyn called to say she had come to a turning point in her life, had left her job with a bank in Denver, was considering moving to New Mexico and asked if she could visit. Claire said yes, although she doubted they had much in common.

When Evelyn arrived at her door, they went through the dance women in their fifties do when they reunite, looking to see how well the other has aged. One woman's quality of life is reflected immediately in the other woman's eyes. The process reminded Claire of the way dogs sniffed each other. The method was more subtle, but she supposed the object was the same — to evaluate the power of the competition.

Claire saw immediately that Evelyn's life was not going well. She had put on weight and wore a baggy brown dress. Her hair was bleached blond, a color that did not become her. The stiffness of her upper lip suggested she'd been deeply wounded or had had a collagen implant. At the same time, Evelyn's eyes implied that Claire didn't look too bad. She still wore a size ten. She had a good hairdresser. Her hair looked frosted rather than bleached to death. But more important than her hair or her weight was that her children were doing well and she had landed on her feet in a place and in a job that she loved. During the turbulence of her divorce her friend Madelyn had handed her a mantra that Claire would always cherish. "You know who you are," Madelyn had said. "You know what you have accomplished."

"Look at *you*." Evelyn stepped back and held Claire at arm's length. "Aren't *you* doing well?"

Claire didn't consider it a triumph to be doing better than Evelyn, but she couldn't help being aware of the fact. Evelyn stayed for a few awkward days, and Claire never heard from her again. She didn't know that Evelyn had moved to Santa Fe. Evelyn would have had the means and opportunity to rob her and quite possibly the motive of needing money. Claire had left her alone in her house all day when she went to work at the Center for Southwest Research at the University of New Mexico. Yet she had found it hard to believe that someone she knew in college would steal from her, and she never told Officer Deutsch about Evelyn's visit.

From the police's point of view, identity fraud was a victimless crime. The credit card companies passed the loss on to their customers in the form of higher interest rates and fees. In Albuquerque, the police dealt with far worse crimes every day. Claire didn't lose much money, but she resented the time and effort it took to get her good credit rating back, listening to bad music while waiting for an overworked employee to come to the phone, the endless hassling once she was able to connect with a human being. She was left with a sense of having been violated, that a slot canyon had formed in her soul. Now that the thief gave every appearance of being Evelyn Martin, the canyon had the potential to flood and turn treacherous.

Claire went into the guest room where Evelyn had slept and where the nightgown lay folded up in a bureau drawer. She took it out and held it in front of her before a full-length mirror. It was the glossy black of cat hair with cleavage that went nearly to her navel. It appeared to conform to the shape of Claire's body, but she couldn't imagine ever wearing it. On the other hand, she couldn't imagine Evelyn wearing it either. Evelyn had always been an inconspicuous person.

A long-forgotten memory came to her as she peered in the mirror. She was in the sorority house dressing for a party and trying on a scoop-necked black dress that belonged to her friend Lynn. The dress, which was too tight, pushed up her breasts and created the illusion that she was stacked.

Evelyn walked by and stopped in the doorway. "Look at you. You have cleavage!" she said with more than a touch of envy.

As Claire recalled, it was the time right before she went to Europe when she was beginning to discover her sexuality. As she folded the nightgown and put it back in the drawer, the thought occurred to her that the theft might have been motivated by envy as well as financial need. It wasn't a thought that Claire was comfortable with, and she folded it up and put it away with the nightgown.

Chapter Two

On the day of the appointment with Detective Amaral, Claire spent the morning in her office at the Center for Southwest Research. At ten her coworker Ruth O'Connor stopped by to ask what she was doing for lunch.

"I'm going to Santa Fe," Claire replied.

"Oh?" asked Ruth, cocking her head.

Ruth had an inquisitive nature and Claire knew she wouldn't be satisfied until she found out exactly why she was going to Santa Fe. "I have an appointment with a detective there," she said.

"A detective?" Ruth's eyes brightened behind her thick glasses. "Have you committed a crime?"

Claire paused for a minute watching her friend, knowing that Ruth was already speculating about the type of crime.

"A woman I knew in college was found dead in her house in Santa Fe. No one missed her until the mailman reported mail piling up in her mailbox."

Ruth, who also lived alone, shivered. "It's not the way I would want to die."

"Me neither."

"Does the detective know what caused her death?"

"Not yet."

Ruth tilted her head and peered through the point in her trifocal lenses where the middle distance was sharp. "Why does he want to talk to you?"

Claire hadn't told anyone about the credit card connection yet, but she knew that eventually she would have to and she might as well begin now. "Because credit cards with my name on them were found in the woman's house."

"Stolen?"

"Issued fraudulently."

"Do you have a lawyer?" Ruth asked.

"Why on earth would I need a lawyer?"

"If the woman was murdered, you would have a motive."

"You're letting your imagination run away with you. There's no reason to believe Evelyn was murdered," Claire replied, but while she said it she had a sense of dark excitement similar to the feeling she'd had when she opened the Victoria's Secret box, an element of fear mingled with the sense that there were dimensions to life that she hadn't begun to explore yet.

In New Mexico spring is the windy

season. The winds were churning on the day Claire drove to Santa Fe, reminding her of children who had been cooped up too long and were running wild with their freedom. Gusts turned her pickup truck into a jittery horse, and she had to hold tight to the steering wheel to keep it from bolting into the fast lane. She got off the interstate at Cerrillos Road and drove to Camino Entrada where the police station was located.

The policewoman at the desk gave directions to Detective Amaral's spartan office. He stood when Claire entered the room and she saw immediately that he was several inches taller than she was. He was young and had a deferential manner. He wore wire-rimmed glasses and his hair stood up in a brush cut that gave him a quality of alertness.

"Thank you for coming," he said in a soft voice that insisted the listener concentrate. "Be seated, please. I hope you had a pleasant drive."

"It was quite windy," Claire said.

"What is it you do in Albuquerque?"

"I am a librarian at the Center for Southwest Research at UNM."

"Ah," said the detective, appearing to make a mental note of this fact and store it away for future reference. "You knew Evelyn Martin in school?"

"Yes. We were classmates at the University of Arizona."

"She is a hard person to place. We can't find any next of kin. Does she have any family, husband or ex-husband, children?"

"Not that I am aware of. She seemed to be living a solitary life. I didn't know her well, but I had the sense she was looking for herself." She supposed from Amaral's startled expression that he didn't know middle-aged people went looking for themselves.

"Are you familiar with any of these names" — the detective glanced at a list on his desk — "Ginny Bogardus, Lynn Granger, or Elizabeth Best?"

"I know all of them," Claire replied. "We were in the same sorority at the U of A." The right phrase, she supposed, was sorority sisters, but she couldn't bring herself to say it.

"We also found credit cards in their names in Evelyn Martin's house."

Claire felt that Detective Amaral was gauging her reaction. "Did she steal their identities, too?" she asked.

"Apparently."

Claire knew that Evelyn's body had been found in a wealthy neighborhood. "Did our good credit buy her a house on Tano Road?"

"No. She was renting. Tell me about your experience with the credit card fraud. Did you file a police report?"

"Yes, with Officer Susan Deutsch from the Albuquerque Police Department."

Amaral wrote down the policewoman's name and listened carefully while Claire told him all about the theft.

"Did you lend Evelyn a key when she visited you?"

"Yes," Claire admitted.

Amaral didn't need to point out that Evelyn could have copied the key and entered her house at any time after her visit. Claire's mind had made that leap already. "How long had she been living in Santa Fe?" she asked.

"She moved here a year ago January."

Claire, who felt that the walls of the slot canyon were closing in on her, pressed her hand against her forehead. "Evelyn lied when she visited me. She told me she was living in Denver and *thinking* about moving here."

"She signed the lease on the house sixteen months ago. In an envelope along with the credit cards we found a list of personal property. Some of it was found in the house. Are you missing any personal property?"

Claire had a few pieces of valuable family

jewelry, but she either wore them daily or kept them in her safe-deposit box. "Not that I know of."

"There is a book on the list. *The Confidence-Man* by Herman Melville."

Claire owned a signed first edition of *The Confidence-Man*. The few books with Melville's signature were valuable. "I have a copy of that book. I hadn't noticed it was missing, but it's possible. It's worth about ten thousand dollars."

"That much for a book?" Amaral's raised eyebrows contributed to his already startled expression.

"That much. Was the book in the house?"

"We didn't find it there. You told me merchandise was charged to your credit card, but you didn't say what it was."

"A large TV, an expensive stereo. Things I never would have bought for myself."

"Anything else?"

"She charged lingerie and underwear at Victoria's Secret. The first sign I had that something was wrong was when I received a package in the mail from the store."

"What was in it?"

"A silky black nightgown."

"Would you be willing to look at a photograph of the deceased?" Amaral asked. "The body is badly decomposed. It will not be a pleasant sight, but you might see something that will help our investigation."

"If the body was decomposed, how were you able to identify her?"

"Dental records matched."

Claire took the photo, which showed a disturbing image of swollen and rotting flesh sprawled across a kitchen floor. The corner of a stove was visible. Evelyn wore a turquoise blue dress with ethnic embroidery. Her hair was bleached blond. While Claire studied the photo, Amaral studied her.

"Evelyn's hair was blond," she said, returning the photo. "That's all I can really identify. Have you discovered yet what killed her?" Claire was thinking a heart attack or possibly a stroke. Evelyn was young for either of those, but she had been overweight and out of shape when she visited Claire.

"Not yet. The OMI needs to do some further testing." Amaral stood up. "Thank you for your time. May I call you if we need to talk further?"

"Of course," Claire said.

She felt numb as Amaral escorted her down the hall to the door. Telephones were ringing in the police station and people were talking, but she barely heard them. She was relieved to step outside into a clear Santa Fe day. The City Different was fifteen hundred feet higher than Albuquerque. The sunlight was even brighter here, giving the shadows deeper definition.

Chapter Three

Claire walked across the parking lot, let herself into her truck and sat down behind the steering wheel, grateful for the familiar shelter of the cab. She wasn't ready to drive back to Albuquerque and considered what to do next. Ginny Bogardus lived in Santa Fe. Claire saw her a few times when she first moved to New Mexico and had been to her house near Acequia Madre. She circled downtown Santa Fe on Paseo de Peralta, turned onto Acequia Madre and off it again onto Ginny's bumpy dirt road. In Santa Fe the better the neighborhood the worse the road. Ginny lived in an excellent neighborhood, close to the Plaza and full of old adobe houses. Claire had once heard it described as an adobe theme park, and it did have a too-perfect-to-be-true quality. But the lilacs were in bloom, the wind ruffled the blossoms, and today the neighborhood had the prettiness-in-motion appearance of an impressionist painting.

She parked in the driveway, walked to the front door and rang the bell. Ginny answered with a glass in one hand and a cigarette in the other. It was only two-thirty in the afternoon, too early to be drinking in Claire's opinion, but she knew that since she'd gotten divorced and moved to Santa Fe, Ginny had lived her life to the accompaniment of ice tinkling in a glass. It was one reason Claire avoided her. Ginny wore a flowered shift that concealed any weight gain. Her hair was layered in an expensive cut and tinted the color of champagne.

"Clairier," she cried. Ginny had nicknames for all her friends, even for people who weren't her friends. "Isn't it just *too* wonderful?"

"Isn't *what* wonderful?" Claire responded.

"That Evie ripped us off and died, and now we're being investigated by Dante. I *love* it!"

Claire thought that Ginny had to be starved for excitement if she found this wonderful, but all she said was, "Dante? You mean Detective Amaral?"

"That's him. *Muy suave,* don't you think? I called the police the minute I saw in the paper that Evelyn had died. He invited me to his office yesterday. I suppose that's why you're in town?"

"It is."

"Come in."

Claire followed her into the house, which

was surprisingly neat considering the carelessness with which Ginny lived. It was decorated with polished antiques and shiny silver. They got as far as a spindly legged antique table in the hallway, where Ginny stopped to rub her cigarette out in an already full ashtray.

"What did Evie steal from you?" she asked.

"My identity."

"She took all of our identities, or tried to. I mean what did she take from your house that you cared about?"

"A book apparently. Herman Melville's *The Confidence-Man*."

"You always did love books, didn't you? I think she wanted to take something we all loved and identified with. I'm partial to jewelry myself, but the jewelry she took was an antique necklace that belonged to my ex-husband's mother. It was pretty, but it wasn't all that valuable. I didn't miss it. I thought I had hidden it well in a fake head of lettuce in my refrigerator, but she found it. Dante described a necklace he discovered in Evie's house that I was sure was mine. When I looked in the lettuce I saw that she had replaced the one I had with a cheap imitation. He said I could have the original back once the investigation was over."

"Why did she want to take something we valued?"

Ginny shrugged. "She identified with us from the past. She wanted to get even with us in the present because we were doing better than she was. Her life was pretty miserable. We had a couple of drinks one night and she told me she'd developed a major crush on her boss, who didn't reciprocate. He was married, of course. She got fired and she couldn't find another job. I think she was also suffering from a hormonal imbalance. We're at that age, aren't we? I told Evie she ought to start taking Premarin. Are you?" Ginny focused on Claire over the rim of her glass.

"No. Are you?"

"Sure. I'll take whatever helps. Evie told me she had enough money to retire on, but she had to have been lying about that. Did she send you a nightgown from Victoria's Secret?"

"Yes."

"I suppose that was some kind of message that she'd been in our house and had the goods on us. I didn't pick up on it, did you?"

"No. I found it hard to believe that someone I knew in college would rip me off."

"Me, too, especially Evie. She was too

boring to be a thief. My nightgown was shocking pink. It was a size fourteen. Did you try yours on?"

"No."

"I did. It made me look like a bottle of Pepto-Bismol. How did Evie know I wore a size fourteen?"

Claire wondered about that since the flowered dress concealed the details of Ginny's figure. "She looked in your closet?"

"Of course. You always were smart. What color was your nightgown?"

"Black."

"Did you notice the turquoise blue dress Evie wore in the police photo? Awful color with that bleached hair. She'd gone ethnic. A lot of women do that when they come to Santa Fe."

"I didn't pay much attention. I was so appalled by the state of the body."

"Gruesome," Ginny agreed and lit another cigarette.

"Did you know Evelyn was living in Santa Fe?"

Ginny shook her head and the ice in her glass trilled an arpeggio. "No. When she visited me about a year ago, she told me she was thinking of moving here. Then I never heard from her again. It was months before she started using my credit cards. I didn't connect her with the theft until I talked to Dante."

"You didn't tell me that Evelyn had visited."

"You didn't tell me either, did you?" she asked. "Actually I did call you, but you didn't call me back. I suppose you were busy with your job and your life in Albuquerque. What was to talk about anyway? It was all so depressing. Having Evie in my house was like spending the winter in Seattle." Ginny shivered. "My ex and I lived there. It was grim — always raining, always gray. If you ask me Evie was always depressing and she wouldn't do anything about it either. I think she liked being miserable. But then what did she have to be happy about? No job, no money, no children, no love life."

"She didn't have much self-esteem," Claire agreed. It was easy enough for a woman to fall into that trap in a society where women were encouraged to dwell on their age and their weight, convinced they needed to buy more to feel better.

"Me, when I get depressed, I pop a Prozac," Ginny said.

Claire recognized this as the moment to give a lecture saying Prozac wasn't meant to be popped whenever you were in a bad mood. To be effective it had to be taken every day, and it should never be taken with alcohol, the mother in her wanted to scold. But she kept quiet and the moment passed.

"Did Dante tell you who else she stole from?" Ginny asked.

"Lynn Granger and Elizabeth Best. Why the four of us?"

"We all lived in the same corridor back then. Maybe she felt closer to us than we thought. It could also be that she intended to rip off all the sisters and got to us first. Then someone ended that little plan. You're still friends with Lynn, aren't you?"

"Yes."

"She's too nice to kill anyone, don't you think? But Lizzie? She always was a bitch. I've been doing some investigating on my own, and I found out exactly where Evelyn lived on Tano Road. I drove up there after I read the article in the paper, and I saw the police tape around the scene. Would you like to see where she was living on our money?"

"I would," Claire admitted, hoping that looking at the house might somehow explain Evelyn's behavior.

Ginny reached for the car keys that were lying in a porcelain dish on the hall table.

Claire stopped her. "I'll drive," she said.

Ginny sat in the passenger seat smoking and sipping from her glass while Claire negotiated the way to Tano Road, another very desirable place to live. Acequia Madre was buried deep in the heart of town. Tano Road was in the foothills with a spectacular view of Santa Fe, which sparkled like a jewel box when the lights came on in the evening. The house was a sprawling, deceptively simple faux adobe hidden behind juniper bushes. Claire hated to speculate how much it had cost Evelyn to live here. Technically, it wasn't her money that had paid the rent. It was MasterCard and Visa money. In a wider sense, everyone's money. Still, since her good credit had been used, she would have preferred that the money had been invested and not wasted on rent.

The house looked sad and empty. The windows, which were devoid of curtains and blinds, presented a blank face to the world. The fact that someone had died here could make it difficult to find a new tenant, Claire thought. On the other hand, there were New Age types in Santa Fe who might consider it a challenge to exorcise the spirit of the deceased.

Ginny led Claire around the corner of the house to the kitchen, where a large rock lay on the ground beneath the window. Apparently someone had placed it there in order to see in. Ginny climbed onto the rock, but Claire was tall enough to look in without it. She saw the stove and the place on the floor where Evelyn's body had been.

"The last time I was here there was an outline of the body on the floor," Ginny said.

Claire didn't need an outline; the decomposed body was clearly visible in her mind's eye.

Ginny climbed down from the rock and Claire followed her around the house, peering through the other windows. Claire wondered what Evelyn did all day in this house other than scheming to rip off her old friends. Was that enough to occupy her time? The furniture had the bare-boned look of a rental, and there wasn't much of it. Once again Claire regretted that the money hadn't been put to better use. The walls inside the house were totally blank — no photographs of family, friends or pets. There was no artwork. There were no books. When she came across the TV with the enormous screen and the wall full of stereo equipment in the living room, Claire began sinking into a black mood, but Ginny's mood seemed to improve with each room that she inspected. She climbed up and down the rocks that had been placed under the windows without missing a step, even though she was wearing sandals that gave her ankles no support.

"Seen enough?" she asked in a voice that was as relentlessly cheerful as the ice that tinkled in her glass.

"Yes," Claire said. "Evelyn could have died of natural causes."

"Possible," Ginny agreed, although her tone lacked conviction.

Claire got back into her truck feeling that all she had learned from this house was that Evelyn had lived a lonely life. They circled the city on Paseo de Peralta on their way back to Ginny's. When they reached the Gerald Peters Gallery, Ginny asked Claire if she would pull in.

"I don't want you to think I'm doing nothing with my life here except going to gallery openings. I know that's what single women in Santa Fe do, but can you imagine a worse place to find a man than a Santa Fe gallery opening? I have a job."

"Doing what?" Claire asked, honoring Ginny's request and entering the gallery parking lot.

"I write about the art scene for an online site called CultureVulture.com. The Peters

Gallery has a lot of openings, and I cover them all. There's a show of Renata Jennings's abstractions that I wrote about last week. I haven't seen it yet."

"You wrote about a show you haven't seen?"

"I have to. The notice goes up on the Web site before the show opens. Whatever people write about art, it's all bullshit anyway, isn't it? Besides, what can you say about a Renata Jennings painting? It's red or it's black." She laughed. "I'd like to take a look at the exhibit to see if what I said is true."

Ginny stepped out of the truck with her glass in her hand. By now the ice had melted and she'd lost her musical accompaniment.

"You won't be allowed in the Peters Gallery with a glass in your hand," Claire pointed out.

"You're right." Ginny tossed whatever liquid was left on the ground and put the glass back in the truck.

The size and scope of Gerald Peters made it seem more like a museum than a gallery. It was a monument to wealth and to beauty. Claire found herself speaking in hushed tones when she was inside.

Ginny, however, wasn't intimidated, aiming her finger, going "bang, bang" and making snide remarks about cowboy-and-Indian art as she led the way to the gallery that housed the Renata Jennings exhibit. Claire didn't remember her being so rude when she was at the U of A, but she wasn't drinking so much then. Sometimes Claire was amused by her outspoken, drunken honesty. Other times she couldn't wait to get away from it. The loudmouthed excursion through the Gerald Peters Gallery made her want to run. They passed a suede sofa that Claire admired.

"It's worth more than my car," Ginny said.

They reached the exhibit in the rear gallery, minimalist paintings consisting of streaks of red and streaks of black.

"There it is," Ginny said. "Your basic red, your basic black. The very essence of picturelessness. Abstractions are either in the box or out of the box. These are in the box."

"That's artbabble, Ginny," Claire replied.

"It's descriptive, it's now," Ginny protested. "That's what CultureVulture likes."

"If you ask me, the Internet is ruining the English language," the librarian in Claire responded. "Everything is written very fast. Nothing is ever proofread or even spell checked."

"I always spell check my submissions," Ginny replied. Her tone was defensive, but her shoulders sagged and her mouth took a downward turn.

Watching her spirits droop made Claire blame herself for being too critical. Although she was also aware that Ginny took her animation from the bottle and it could be time for a refill.

"Let's get out of here," Ginny said.

Claire drove her home, not making any attempt to get out of her truck when they reached Ginny's house.

"Would you like to come in, have a little drink for the road?" she asked.

"I better not," Claire replied.

"You could have a soda if you don't want a real drink." She stared at her fingernails, which Claire noticed had been chewed ragged. "I always feel down at this time of day, when darkness is coming on."

"The night skies in New Mexico are so beautiful. Do you ever go out and look at the stars?" Claire asked. "It might make you feel better about darkness and night."

"No," Ginny said, putting her hand on the door. "Sure you don't want to come in?"

It won't be any easier to leave later than it is now, Claire thought. "I better go."

"Okay," Ginny said. "Nice to see you,

Clairier. Stay in touch."

"You, too," Claire replied.

On the drive back to Albuquerque, it occurred to her that it would have been wiser to have lingered longer. It was the hour when everyone was rushing to get home from work, and the setting sun beamed right in her eyes, magnifying every speck of dust and smashed insect on the windshield. At this hour Claire thought that no matter how carefully you managed to clean the glass, it would never be clean enough.

Chapter Four

When she got home, Nemesis was waiting at the door, expecting to be cuddled and fed.

"Not now," Claire said, skirting the cat and heading for her bedroom, where the walls were lined from ceiling to floor with books. Bookshelves formed a mantel across the doorway and circled the windows. Books were a form of insulation that kept the outer world from disturbing her inner world.

From the doorway she could see that there were no empty places on her shelves. If *The Confidence-Man* had been stolen, it had been replaced by another book. She went to the *M*'s in her Americana section. *The Confidence-Man* was exactly where it belonged, but as she reached for the shelf, she saw that it was not her copy. This book was the Oxford World's Classics edition with a critical introduction and explanatory notes, twenty-five years old and worthless.

"Goddamn it," Claire said.

It could be an expensive loss, but she insured her valuable books and expected the insurance company to cover it. It wasn't the value of the book or the loss of it that bothered her most. What disturbed Claire deeply was that Evelyn Martin had violated her sanctuary. She could get over someone wantonly using her credit cards. It was harder to get over a classmate and houseguest entering her bedroom and stealing from her.

Claire was becoming ever more convinced that Evelyn's motive went beyond financial need. There were other valuable items in her house and in Ginny's. Evelyn had gone to the trouble to replace her book and Ginny's jewelry, but she did it with poor imitations that would be obvious as soon as the victims went to the trouble to look for them. She seemed to be taunting her old friends, and there was a level of chicanery going on that might have amused her. *The Confidence-Man* was the story of a con artist with a constantly shifting identity who traveled the Mississippi on a riverboat ripping off the other passengers. Evelyn had been acting as a confidence woman herself by conning Claire while she robbed her house. But Claire had never seen much humor in Evelyn Martin, and she hadn't seen much confidence either.

She might well have been motivated by envy and anger, feelings fueled by despair and an empty life. "Look at *you*," she had said to Claire. *"You're* doing so well." In a financial sense Claire *was* doing well. Her salary at CSWR was modest, but she had an inheritance and she had investments. She didn't have a devoted man in her life, but she no longer had the drain of an unfaithful one either. Her work, her friends and her children gave her satisfaction and joy, but she had created that situation herself by taking careful steps moment by moment, day by day. To quote one of her favorite poems, "acting in the little ways that encourage good fortune." Claire liked to believe that people were handed a piece of clay at birth, although not the same piece of clay. Some got a piece that was more malleable. Some got more clay than others. But everyone's task was to make the best sculpture she possibly could out of her piece.

At that task Evelyn had failed miserably. Not only had she died unmissed and unmourned, but she had left a mess of deceit behind. All that she had created from her clay was bitterness and envy. Claire supposed that sooner or later the other victims would reach the same conclusion she had — Evelyn robbed them because on one level she envied them and on another level she hated them.

She sank into an armchair with *The*

41

Confidence-Man on her lap. It wasn't one of her favorite Melville books. She bought it years ago because signed editions were rare, and she knew it to be a good value. Over the years it had been appreciating on her shelves. If she was going to actually read Melville, she preferred *Billy Budd, Sailor* and *Bartleby the Scrivener. The Confidence-Man* was too metaphysical to be popular and it turned out to be the last book Melville published in his lifetime. *Billy Budd* was published posthumously. Eventually Melville went to work in the customs house and all of his books were out of print when he died. Recognition and success came after his death, a story that could give a writer nightmares.

Claire glanced at the book, which had fallen open to an introduction by a critic named Jeffrey Omer that was full of pompous phrases. At first glance the phrases appeared to be loaded with meaning, but on closer examination they turned out to be critical double-talk that resembled Ginny's artbabble. She saw Omer as another con artist creating a smokescreen with empty phrases.

It made Claire long for simplicity, clarity and sleep. She knew she would have bad dreams if she went to bed with that book on her shelf and the feeling that her bedroom was full of tricksters. She took it down the hall and left it in her office.

It was customary in New Mexico to burn a smudge stick made of dried sage to drive bad thoughts from a house. Claire lit one and walked through the house, inhaling the fragrant smell. She left the sage burning in a dish in the bedroom while she fed Nemesis and prepared dinner for herself. When it was time to go to bed, the bedroom was thick with smoke. Claire opened the windows to clear the room. Eventually she fell asleep and dreamed she saw a ghostly figure in a turquoise dress pulling books from her shelves then throwing them to the floor in an angry fit. She woke up knowing it would take more than smudge sticks to rid herself of the nightmare of Evelyn Martin.

In the morning she learned of another death when her daughter, Robin, called to tell her "Nana died."

Nana was Claire's former mother-in-law and Robin's grandmother. "I'm sorry," Claire replied. She had never been close to the mother-in-law, who had kept her son's affections on a short leash, but Nana had been a devoted grandmother to Claire's children.

"She died in her sleep," Robin said. "They think it was a heart attack. Dad is *so* upset."

"I'm sure he is, dear."

"The funeral is Saturday. Dad wants me to come, but I have a paper due Monday."

Robin lived in Boston and was getting a master's degree at Harvard.

"Would you go for me, Mom?"

"I don't know, Robin. I'm not a part of the family anymore. Your father has a new wife."

"Oh, Melissa," Robin sighed.

Listening to Robin complain about Melissa was a guilty pleasure, but one Claire was ashamed to indulge in.

"Eric can't go either. He's got a conference coming up," Robin said.

Eric was Claire's son, who worked in the computer business in Silicon Valley.

"Someone who knew Nana when we were growing up should go. She was a good grandmother to us. You know she was, Mom. Please go."

"All right," Claire said.

"Would you take care of the flowers for Eric and me?"

"Yes, dear."

"Thank you so much, Mom. You're the best."

Claire got off the phone wondering if

she'd been conned by her own daughter and trying to remember how old Nana had been. Eighty-five? To die in one's sleep of a heart attack at that age was not a bad death. It was sad, but it was inevitable. The death of people her own age or younger was not inevitable. Angry as she was at Evelyn, she still felt sadness at the circumstances of her death. She would do her duty and go to Nana's funeral, staying as distant from Evan and his new wife, Melissa, as she possibly could. Once that chore was over she intended to visit Elizabeth Best in Tucson and Lynn Granger in Cave Creek.

She did her tai chi practice and then she called Lynn, who had been divorced twice and might be able to advise her on the etiquette of dealing with the funeral of a former mother-in-law.

"Let me think," Lynn said. "One of my mothers-in-law died before I married her son. I don't know what happened to the other one. We lost touch. I guess she's still around somewhere. Do you think it's possible to go on caring about the mother of someone you divorced?"

"Possible," Claire said. "But the reason I'm going is because my daughter asked me to."

"It should be fun to see Evan and Melissa again," was Lynn's sarcastic reply.

"Um," said Claire, "has Detective Amaral been in touch with you about Evelyn Martin's death?"

"He has and he told me about the credit card fraud. According to him she stole all of our identities. Apparently she didn't feel she had one of her own."

"Did she send you a nightgown, too?"

"Yup. It was lavender, size sixteen. It fit, I'm sorry to say, but can you see me in a lavender nightgown from Victoria's Secret? It would give Steve another heart attack."

"Did you connect the credit card fraud with Evelyn before Amaral called?"

"No. It happened so long after her visit, and she *was* our sorority sister, after all. Steve always suspected her, though. He didn't much like Evelyn. He thinks her motive was envy."

"That's what I came up with."

"Okay, she envied you because you have two wonderful children, an interesting job and you're independent. Why me? Because I have Steve?"

Lynn did have an enviable marriage, Claire knew. On her third try she had gotten it right. "You also live in a beautiful place."

"True. But what did she envy about

Ginny? From what I hear she's drunk most of the time."

"Well, she came out of her divorce with enough money to live in Santa Fe. She has a job, but she doesn't have to work. Why Elizabeth?"

"That's easy. She has a young lover. Stop by and meet him when you are in Tucson. It'll be worth the trip. You're going to visit us while you're in Arizona, aren't you?"

"Of course."

"See you soon," Lynn said.

When Claire got to her office at CSWR, she contacted the appropriate rare book dealers to tell them that her *Confidence-Man* had been stolen. There weren't many dealers in the country who dealt in books of that caliber, and *Confidence-Man* was likely to make its way to one of them, although it might pass through the hands of several other dealers first. A thief who didn't know its value might well sell it cheap, but Evelyn had been calculating enough that Claire believed she would have gone to the trouble to find out what the objects she stole were worth before selling them. She spoke to three of her favorite dealers: Tom Butterworth in Denver, Simon Collins in New York and Brett Moon in Los Angeles.

None of them had heard anything about the book, which rather surprised Claire. Since *Confidence-Man* had not been found in Evelyn's house, she assumed Evelyn had sold it and spent the money.

All of the dealers promised to call Claire if the book turned up, and she trusted them enough to believe they would. Brett Moon was in a talkative mood. Claire had known him for years and she visualized him as they talked. As time went by and his head became pale and bald as a full moon, he grew into his surname.

"I didn't know you had a *Confidence-Man*," he said.

"I've owned it for years. I bought it when I was still at the U of A."

"Did your boss know about it?"

"Unlikely. I can't think of any reason I would tell him about it." Claire spoke to her pompous and prickly boss, Harrison Hough, as little as possible. She had to talk to him about library books. She didn't have to talk to him about her personal collection.

"He collects Melville. Did you know that?"

"No."

"He did his doctoral dissertation on Melville. He's always asking me to find signed first editions for him. He would have wanted to buy yours if he'd known you had one."

Claire was glad she hadn't mentioned it. The last person she would have wanted to sell her book to was Harrison Hough.

"I'll call you immediately if it turns up here," Brett said.

"Thanks," Claire replied.

A book Harrison coveted had been stolen from her bedroom. Evelyn was the obvious culprit, but even if she were not, Claire would never have suspected Harrison. If he was capable of stealing anything it was his employees' joy and spirit, not their books. As if to prove her point — or make her feel guilty for the thoughts she'd had — he walked by her office wearing a sour expression. She turned her back to the window that faced the hallway and dialed Detective Amaral's number.

"I checked when I got home and found *The Confidence-Man* was gone," she told him. "Evelyn replaced it with a worthless critical edition. I called the places where the book is likely to turn up, but none of the dealers have seen it yet. They all promised to call me if they do see it."

"Do you trust them?" Amaral asked in his soft, precise voice.

"I do. There aren't very many people who

deal in books of this caliber, and they all know each other. Reputation is everything. It seems strange to me that the book hasn't shown up yet, if Evelyn stole it when she was in my house."

"Do you know that she took it then?" Amaral answered. "If she copied your key, she could have come back for it at any time."

"Have you found out yet what caused her death?" Claire asked to fill the depression caused by the detective's remark.

"Yes," he said. "There was a single blunt force trauma to the skull."

"Oh, no," Claire replied. "What kind of a blunt instrument was used?"

"That hasn't been established yet. I may wish to talk to you further."

"Of course," she said. When she got off the phone she had the sense that a storm that had been building in the distance was moving closer to her narrow canyon.

On Friday afternoon Claire left for Tucson. It was a drive she enjoyed, full of wide-open spaces and light that shifted from moment to moment. In full daylight the mountains south of Albuquerque appeared to be gray wolves loping toward Mexico. Clouds crossing the sun dappled their backs with shadow. At sunset these mountains turned a radiant rosé. Interstate 25 passed by Elephant Butte, where the Rio Grande had been dammed to form a lake. The water reflected the pale sky as it drifted in and out of view between the mesas.

She turned southwest onto State Highway 26 at Hatch, the town that billed itself as the chile capital of the world. At this time of year farmers were plowing the fields and stirring up clouds of dust. Claire was glad to escape from the dust as she continued southwest on the emptiness of Highway 26. At Deming she turned onto I-10, the southern route to California. It was not as popular with truckers as I-40, the middle route, which made for easier driving. It was also an airplane route and the sky was crisscrossed with white contrails.

As she approached the Arizona border, Claire drove through some of her favorite open spaces in the Southwest. The vastness here left room for wandering thoughts, and hers turned to the death of Evelyn Martin and to her old friends Ginny, Lynn and Elizabeth. Was it possible one of them had murdered Evelyn? She didn't think any of them were capable of cold-blooded murder, but one of them might have discovered that Evelyn had robbed her and stolen her identity. Suppose she went to the house on Tano Road to confront the thief? Evelyn attacked, the woman picked up the blunt object — there was sure to be one in a kitchen — to defend herself. Claire hadn't spoken to Elizabeth yet. Ginny and Lynn hadn't admitted to connecting Evelyn with the theft before Amaral called, but it was possible one of them was lying.

Other than some hard summer rains and an occasional lightning strike, there wasn't much weather in this part of the country. Tornadoes, snowstorms or floods were all possible but very rare. Usually the sky was so clear that Claire had an unobstructed view of the mountains and the plains, but today the wind raised dust devils in the distance. Even if she couldn't see the effect of the wind, she could feel it in the rebellious behavior of her truck.

She entered Arizona feeling a sadness that this state was no longer home. She loved New Mexico, but there was a time when she had loved Arizona as much or more. She had spent twenty-eight years in Arizona with Evan Burch. She knew his every mood, and she knew that he would feel abandoned by his mother's death. Evan was an only child, and no one would ever love him the way his mother had. He would be reaching out for comfort. Well, that was Melissa's job now. All Claire had to do was show up and try to be civil.

She had entered farming country again. The wind lifted dust devils from newly plowed fields and marched them toward I-10 like an advancing army. Wind was the one natural disaster capable of turning I-10 treacherous. Claire had been so preoccupied with her thoughts about family and friends that she had forgotten about the danger of driving through this part of the country in the spring when the fields were freshly plowed and the winds were high. An army of dust swept across the highway and enveloped her truck. She clutched the steering wheel, stepped on the brake, turned on her headlights and her emergency lights, but it was too little, too late.

She could see nothing but brown dust. She knew there was a semi behind her and a compact car in front of her, but they had disappeared from view. Sound gave her no guidance; all she could hear was the howl of the wind. The cloud was so thick she might not see vehicles until the instant before she crashed into them, even if their headlights and brake lights were on. It was tempting to pull over, but that would make her a sitting target. If she kept moving, however slowly, she would eventually get through this. Claire knew that this kind of windstorm could cause pileups involving dozens of cars. She turned off the tape deck to give her full attention to the road, but she couldn't turn off the tape that played in her mind. How close was the semi behind her? Should she pull over? Should she stop? She began to feel that the dust had entered her brain, and that if she didn't lose her life in this dust storm, she would surely lose her mind.

She came up suddenly on the flashing lights of the car ahead of her and pressed down hard on her brakes, hoping the semi wasn't still on her tail. The car's lights became a beacon that guided her through the storm. She stayed a respectful distance, not too close to stop in time, not far enough away to lose sight of the lights. The car was her guide, but if it drove off the road into a ditch she would too. Sometimes dust gusted between the cars and she lost sight of it, but then the lights blinked on again.

Slowly the dust began to lift. She was able to ascertain the color of the car — yellow. There was a last gust of wind and they had driven through the storm. The driver stepped on the gas and sped ahead. Claire looked in her rearview mirror and saw the semi breathing down her neck. She was glad she hadn't known how close it was as they passed through the storm. The driver swung into the fast lane, flashed his lights, honked his horn and waved as he passed, letting her know that she had been the beacon for him.

Chapter Five

The funeral was held in the Episcopal church Evan's family had stopped attending years before. It was, in fact, the church in which Claire and Evan got married, a stone building with stained-glass windows that made no concessions to its desert location. To Claire it appeared to have been transported intact from the Midwest, as had many of its parishioners. The first time she saw this church, she had an image of it sprouting wings and flying to Tucson from a suburb on Chicago's North Shore. Compulsive as she was about being on time, she somehow managed to arrive at the church ten minutes late. She had spent the night with her friend Madelyn and they had lingered over coffee. Some people might consider showing up late a lapse in character, but for Claire it was a small victory, late enough to allow her to take a seat in the rear of the church behind everyone else. There were more people than she would have expected at the funeral of an eighty-five-year-old woman, but Nana had remained active in the community and lived at home until the end. She had been married to Paul, Claire's former father-in-law, for sixty years, and Claire knew he would not be taking this well.

While the minister spoke to the accompaniment of organ music and sobs, Claire stared at the flower arrangements on the altar, wondering which one had come from her and the children, thinking that Nana had lived a life full of family and volunteerism. The service was mercifully short. The mourners stood up. The family began walking down the aisle. Evan came first with his father hanging on his arm. Paul had aged since Claire last saw him. His posture was stooped and he had a shuffling walk. Evan's hair fell across his forehead in little-boy bangs. His face was swollen and his eyes were red. She couldn't remember ever seeing him cry during all the years she'd been married to him. Melissa followed Evan and Paul with every blond hair in place and wearing a black dress that looked expensive. She had put on weight, about ten pounds in Claire's judgment. Not enough to make her look frumpy, but enough to send the signal that she was no longer in the market. Was that a sign of contentment, Claire wondered, or unhappiness? Weight gain could be either. It was hard to judge at a funeral where one was expected to be unhappy.

She followed the rest of the mourners out of the church and waited on line to offer condolences. She came to Paul first. Claire had never felt close to him; he was a man who stayed in the background and let his wife perform all the social functions. Yet he seemed pleased to see her.

"Claire," he said, taking her hand. "It's so good of you to come. Nana was fond of you, and the children were always her pride and joy."

"She was a wonderful grandmother to them," Claire replied.

Up close she could see that Evan had also aged. He still looked like a preppy, but his hair seemed thinner and grayer, and he had put on a few pounds, too, leading Claire to wonder if Melissa liked to cook. While Evan gave Claire a stiff hug, she glanced over his shoulder and saw his new wife standing farther down the sidewalk talking to people her own age.

"Thanks for coming," Evan said. "I wish the children were here."

"I'm sorry, Evan," Claire said, summoning as much warmth as she could. "I know how much your mother meant to you."

"We're inviting friends and family back to Dad and Mother's house after. Could you come?"

"I'll try," Claire said.

"I hear you're doing well at the center," Evan said.

"I like New Mexico," she replied. "And you? How are things at the U of A?"

"All right. I . . ." The expression in his eyes was skirting dangerously close to an abyss of regret. If he had any regrets, Claire didn't want to hear them. There were people in line behind her. It was time to move on.

"I hope we'll see you later," Evan said.

Claire made a wide circle around Melissa and her friends as she walked to her truck. It was the only truck among the SUVs and sedans in the church parking lot, which seemed symbolic of the fact that she had started a new life in a rougher place. She got into the cab considering what to do next. She wasn't sure whether it was an ex-wife's duty to go back to the house or not. It might make the new wife uncomfortable. It would certainly make the old wife uncomfortable.

Instead of driving toward the house in the foothills where she had spent many a dull holiday eating overcooked turkey and mashed potatoes, she drove to the U of A and parked in front of the sorority house. It also looked like a transplant from another place, a place with tradition and deciduous trees, a place with cats and dogs, a place that wasn't surrounded by mountains and desert, coyotes and rattlesnakes. The sorority was housed in a three-story brick building with white shutters.

It embarrassed Claire now that she had ever been a member of a sorority. She was reluctant to enter the building, but she forced herself. There had been some changes over the years. The insipid blue carpeting had been replaced (thank God) by polished floors and scatter rugs. The upholstered furniture was in the overstuffed, subdued-color mode popular now. Still the overall effect was as bland and soothing as it had been when she lived there. The polished furniture and pastel upholstery created a false sense of security. At this point in life Claire thought it was better to recognize that the world was a dangerous place and to deal with that reality. Although she could hear music playing upstairs, no one was in sight. Claire had no desire to encounter anybody; she considered this a solo expedition. There was a box in the entryway with a sign on it that read "Donate your old clothes to Goodwill."

It was a tradition that had endured over the years and evoked in Claire the memory of a nasty scene she had witnessed over clothes in that box when she lived in this house. It wouldn't be the same box after all this time but another one dedicated ironically to Goodwill. She remembered Elizabeth Best coming across a sorority sister named Miranda Kohl wearing her jacket. It was an unusually cold and blustery day and they were on the street when the incident happened. Elizabeth had a mean temper. She grabbed Miranda by the arm and demanded that she take off the jacket. In the style of the sixties, Miranda liked to wear outfits she bought at thrift stores. She had a mane of copper-colored curls and a flawless complexion and looked good in fringe and long denim skirts as well as in an expensive suede jacket. Miranda claimed in her rather spacey way that she found the jacket in the Goodwill box and she thought that whoever it belonged to didn't want it anymore. She shouldn't have taken clothes from that box, but Miranda didn't have much money and the sisters tended to look the other way if she showed up in their discarded clothes.

Elizabeth insisted she hadn't discarded the jacket, that it had been stolen from her closet. She claimed she had reported the theft to Mrs. Rutherford, the housemother. Mrs. R heard the commotion and came outside. Followed by several sisters, she went upstairs to Miranda's room and began yanking clothes off hangers in the back of her closet, clothes that had all been stolen from the girls in the sorority.

"I didn't put those clothes there," Miranda cried.

To Claire's inexperienced eye she appeared stunned and shocked, but Miranda was also an actress. She was a scholarship student who came from a different background than the other sisters and they were not inclined to believe her. Mrs. R said she wouldn't press charges on the condition that Miranda left the sorority house. Miranda not only left the house, she dropped out of school and pursued an acting career. Claire saw her occasionally in television commercials and in bit parts on TV series. Sometimes she appeared young and glamorous in her commercials, but she also did one for Lemon Pledge in which she appeared as a grandmother. Claire supposed Miranda was paid very well, but she hated to see the Lemon Pledge commercials because the radiant young Miranda she remembered had been made up to look eighty years old.

Her memory of the angry scene involving Miranda and the clothes came back vividly, although she couldn't be sure that it was entirely accurate at this point. There was one point, however, that she was absolutely sure about, which was that Miranda's roommate at the time had been Evelyn Martin. She remembered Evelyn watching with a blank expression while Mrs. R pulled the clothes from the closet. The thought that Evelyn could have framed Miranda back then made Claire dizzy and she headed outside for some fresh air.

As she reached for the front door, it was opened from the outside by two young women.

"Can we help you?" one of them asked.

"I don't think so," Claire replied.

"Are you someone's mother?" asked the other.

"Yes," answered Claire. "But my daughter doesn't live here."

Claire followed her road map to Elizabeth Best's house. She had recently moved back to the Tucson area to be with the new man in her life, a woodworker, and she lived on the outskirts of the city in an area of scrubby desert. When Claire had lived in Tucson, Elizabeth lived in the former mining town of Bisbee, embracing her idea of an alternative lifestyle. As Claire recalled, her significant other at that point was an artist. She saw Elizabeth from time to time during those years. Elizabeth had never married, but as far as Claire knew, she had never been without a man or children. Elizabeth's lifestyle, supported by a sizable trust fund, made room for creative and impoverished men. Many women tried to hitch their stars to men who had power. Elizabeth's money gave her the power and she was capable of abusing it in all the ways that men did.

In the semirural area where she now lived the numbers of the houses weren't clearly marked, so Claire studied the houses themselves trying to guess which one belonged to Elizabeth. She didn't expect it to be ostentatious, but she did expect it to be unique. When she saw a rambling old adobe, she pulled into the driveway. She knew she'd come to the right place when her arrival stirred up a storm of activity. The sleepy, dusty yard turned into a swirl of dust, a cacophony of dogs and children. One of the dogs, a yappy little mutt, nipped at her heels as she stepped out of her truck. A towheaded boy, who appeared to be around eight years old, yelled, *"Cállate, perrito,"* reminding Claire that one of Elizabeth's accomplishments was a fluency in Spanish.

Elizabeth came to the door wearing jeans and a T-shirt and balancing a dark-haired baby on her hip. Could the baby be hers?

Claire wondered. It was possible, if not probable. She would be in her fifties now, although she didn't look it. Elizabeth still had the kind of full-breasted, long-legged body men loved. She was tall and had always had excellent posture. The legs in the faded jeans went on forever. She had allowed some gray to show in her hair, but mostly it was ash blond and she wore it pinned up on top of her head with stray tendrils wrapping around her neck. Elizabeth had been dealt a royal flush at birth that included looks *and* money. To her credit, she had managed to hold on to both. Claire liked to believe that eventually character won out, but she knew that all Elizabeth had to do to win the games she played was to flash her high cards. She was quite capable of doing so if it was to her advantage.

"Claire Reynier?" she called. "Is that you?"

"Hello, Elizabeth," Claire replied.

"Come on in."

Claire tried to get across the yard, but the dog nipping at her heels made it difficult.

"Toby, hold on to Michoacan," Elizabeth yelled.

The boy grabbed the dog and it yapped in protest while Claire made her way to the door.

"Is that *your* baby?" she asked.

"Good God, no. She belongs to Allison, the daughter of my significant other, Jess. We named her Artemis. She's beautiful, don't you think?"

Claire had to admit that she was.

"Toby was my last child."

"By Jess?"

"No, Alan is his father. You met Alan in Bisbee. Do you remember?"

"I'm not sure." It was hard to keep up with the men in Elizabeth's life. "How old is Toby? Eight?"

"Exactly. Come in," she said. "Let's get out of the heat."

It was still spring but already the temperature was heading for triple digits. The interior of the house was cool and dark, decorated in Mexican colors with walls painted deep red or brilliant yellow. Paper cutouts and piñatas were suspended from the ceiling. They entered the kitchen, where a teenage girl was chopping vegetables on the counter. She was lovely, too, but in a different way than Elizabeth. She was small and delicate with dark curly hair and pale-as-moonlight skin. Claire wondered where she fit into the menage but Elizabeth didn't bother with introductions.

"What are you doing, Allison?" she snapped.

"Making gazpacho," the girl replied without looking up from the peppers she was chopping into tiny pieces.

"Don't chop on the counter. Use the cutting board." Elizabeth indicated the butcher block that stood in the middle of the room and was piled high with baby clothes.

"I'm being careful," the girl replied, continuing to chop. "I'm not cutting through to the counter, see?" She demonstrated the precision that allowed her to chop the vegetables without actually cutting into the tile countertop.

"This is my house, Allison," Elizabeth said. "You don't chop vegetables on the kitchen counter in my house."

"You don't need to remind me this is your house," Allison replied.

"*This* is where you chop." With her free arm Elizabeth swept the clothes off the butcher block and onto the floor. Alarmed by the commotion, the baby in her other arm began to fuss.

"It's time for her nap," Allison said, reaching for her daughter.

"I'll put her down," Elizabeth said. "You can clean up the mess in here." She walked out of the room hugging the baby in her arms.

"I'm Claire Reynier," Claire said, breaking an awkward silence and extending her hand to the girl.

"Allison Grady," the girl replied, putting down her knife, wiping her hands on her jeans and shaking Claire's hand.

"Can I help you clean up?" Claire asked.

"I don't need any help," Allison replied. She picked up the vegetables she had chopped, dropped them into the garbage pail, scooped up the baby clothes and walked out of the kitchen mumbling to herself.

Claire followed the path Elizabeth had taken into the next room, which appeared to be the living room. The house wandered as if the rooms had been tacked on at random whenever another one was needed. A golden retriever dozed on an overstuffed brown velvet sofa. A portrait of an elegant woman hung over the fireplace, Elizabeth's mother, an heiress who had preserved her fortune and made her daughter's way of life possible. As Claire recalled it was railroad money. She went to the window, deeply recessed in an adobe wall at least two feet thick, making the house a double adobe, even cooler, even darker. She was watching birds picking at seeds in the garden when Elizabeth returned without the baby. She sat down on the sofa, picked up the dog's head and placed it in her lap. The dog's legs trembled as it chased something in its sleep.

"*Cálmate, perro,*" Elizabeth said.

"Is your mother still alive?" Claire asked.

"She died two years ago," Elizabeth replied.

"My ex-husband's mother just died. One reason I came to Arizona was to go to the funeral."

"How was that?"

"Difficult."

"I suppose you also want to talk to me about Evelyn Martin."

"I do."

"Detective Amaral told me he now believes she was murdered. Does he think one of us killed her?" Her hand stroked the dog's silky back.

"We are the likely suspects," Claire replied.

"Esperanza," Elizabeth called. "Would you get us something to drink?"

A Mexican maid stepped into the room. "Sí, señora." She went to get the drinks.

"I stopped at the sorority house on my way here," Claire said.

"How does it look?"

"The blue carpet is gone."

"Thank God for that," Elizabeth said.

"Being there reminded me of the time you found Miranda Kohl wearing your jacket."

Elizabeth raised her chin and her blue eyes had a hard glimmer. "She stole it from me," she said. "We hardly ever watch television in this house, but when we do and we see that Lemon Pledge commercial, I click it off."

"If she stole it from you, why would she wear it where she might see you?"

Elizabeth shrugged. "She didn't expect to run into me that day. She forgot where she got it from. She was stoned. Miranda was a space case. I'm not surprised she became an actress, but, God, does she have to look so old in that commercial? Nobody could pay me enough to look *that* old."

Esperanza came into the room with two glasses of iced lemonade and placed them on the coffee table.

"Gracias, Esperanza," Elizabeth said. She was kind to maids, pets and children, ruthless to anyone she considered competition. Claire thought it a sign of insecurity to treat a significant other's daughter as competition, but that was one interpretation of the scene in the kitchen.

"Do you remember who Miranda's roommate was at the time?" she asked Elizabeth.

70

"No. I hardly remember who my own roommate was."

"It was Evelyn Martin. I was in the hallway when the housemother pulled the clothes from Miranda's closet. I remember Evelyn standing in the background. It would have been very easy for her to have moved the clothes from her closet to Miranda's, to have given Miranda your jacket or even to have put it in the Goodwill box herself."

"It's possible," Elizabeth said, sipping at her lemonade. "Well, that would supply Miranda with motivation to kill Evelyn, wouldn't it? So why is Detective Amaral bothering us?"

"How would he know about Miranda? And why would Miranda go after Evelyn now when that happened so long ago?"

"Who knows?" Elizabeth asked. She yawned, indicating this conversation had begun to bore her, reminding Claire that she had a short attention span. She picked up a cell phone from the coffee table and cradled it in her hand.

"When did Evelyn visit you?" Claire asked.

"About a year ago. She looked terrible. She told me she was thinking of moving to Tucson, which was a lie since Amaral told me she was already settled in the house in Santa Fe by then. I'm on the board of several environmental organizations. I was busy and I hardly saw her. Jess spent more time with her than I did. He likes stray animals. This dog is one of Jess's strays, but she's a sweet stray. No one would ever accuse Evelyn of being sweet. Boring maybe. Boring may be inconspicuous but it isn't sweet."

"When did you discover that Evelyn had used your credit cards?"

"I didn't until Amaral called me. When the bills showed up, I just assumed Allison was the offender. She's sixteen. She couldn't cope after the baby was born and I took her in. She had problems with drugs. She had access to my mail and credit card offers. I assumed she was selling the stuff she bought or trading it for drugs. Jess didn't want to believe she would do it, but I thought he was in denial. Amaral said I should have reported it to the police right away, but I didn't see the point. I thought it was something we would work out here."

"Did Evelyn steal something you valued from the house?"

"Some of my mother's silver was missing. It had been replaced with silver plate. When

I discovered the switch, I attributed that to Allison, too."

"Was it found in Evelyn's house?"

"Yes. Detective Amaral said I could claim it after the investigation is over. It isn't that valuable, but it was my mother's so it means something to me."

"Did Evelyn send you a nightgown from Victoria's Secret?"

"She did. It was peach colored. Jess liked it." Elizabeth smiled and opened the cell phone.

"Didn't you wonder where it had come from?"

"Not for long. Would you like to meet Jess?" Before Claire could respond, Elizabeth dialed a number. "Sweetie," she said. "I have an old friend here who'd like to meet you. Okay. We'll be right over." She put the phone down and turned to Claire. "He's in his shop. Jess is a fine woodworker."

She lifted the dog's head from her lap and stood up. Claire followed her out the door, across the patio and into Jess's shop. He was standing at a workbench polishing an inlaid wooden bowl. The jeans he wore demonstrated that his legs were as long as Elizabeth's. Jess was Anglo, but he had adopted an Indian look. His black hair was parted in the middle and pulled back into a ponytail.

He wore a silver and turquoise bracelet. It was a strong statement, but Jess was too pale to carry it off. He seemed lacking in energy to Claire. He had to be ten years younger than she and Elizabeth, old enough to have fathered a sixteen-year-old girl, but young to be a grandfather. He would be a trophy in some people's eyes, but not in Claire's. Elizabeth, who had enough drive for two, had the ability to steal other people's life force. It was the price they paid for drifting into her orbit.

Jess showed Claire the bowl he'd been working on. She admired it even though she thought the workmanship was sloppy.

"Claire and I went to college together. She was robbed by Evelyn, too," Elizabeth said.

Jess shook his head. "There was something about Evelyn I didn't trust, but Elizabeth, she trusts everybody."

Claire thought that Jess had to be under Elizabeth's influence to make that statement. In her experience the only people Elizabeth trusted were the people she controlled.

"Now that the police have established Evelyn was murdered, Detective Amaral thinks one of us did it, but you know it wasn't me. I was with you, wasn't I, darling?" Elizabeth put her arm around Jess and leaned her head on his shoulder.

"Of course you were," Jess replied.

"The state of the body makes it impossible to establish the exact time of death," Claire pointed out.

"It doesn't matter. Whenever it was, Jess and I were together," Elizabeth said.

Claire glanced at her watch. "It's been good visiting with you, but I need to go. I'm on my way to Lynn Granger's."

"Give her my best," Elizabeth said.

"Nice meeting you," Jess said.

"You, too," Claire replied.

Chapter Six

As she drove north from Tucson, Claire thought that Elizabeth had to be the kind of woman people meant by the phrase "high maintenance." She demanded obedience and needed constant attention. Claire admired her drive and energy, but not what she did with it. Elizabeth had grown up in a family full of girls and apparently still considered every other female a competitor. Claire sought tranquility, and being around Elizabeth rattled her nerves. The road was full of semis and RVs that contributed to her edgy feeling. Claire remembered when I-10 from Tucson to Phoenix was a pleasant drive through the scrubby desert, but every time she returned to Arizona there were more vehicles on the road, more houses in the foothills, and both continued to increase in size. She looked forward to arriving at Lynn Granger's tranquil home in Cave Creek. To sit on the patio surrounded by saguaros, listening to the coyotes yip and howl, and watch the sunset with her old friend would be a soothing way to end this annoying day. Evan, Melissa and Elizabeth in one day had been too much.

She kept an eye on her rearview mirror, watching Tucson fading into the distance. The view blurred as her eyes filled with tears. What are you crying about? she asked herself. The loss of the past? The death of Nana? Although she hadn't been close to Nana, death was always upsetting. She couldn't be shedding any more tears over Evan and Melissa, could she? She and Evan had been together for twenty-eight years and had raised two children. She had put enough time between her and the divorce by now that she could remember some good times among the bad. She turned on the radio, spun the dial looking for classical music, but settled on Linda Ronstadt.

Although the traffic remained heavy, once Tucson was no longer visible, Claire felt better. She looked forward to visiting Lynn, the one sister she really enjoyed being with. She always followed the same route through Phoenix, taking the Black Canyon Freeway and Cave Creek Road.

Lynn moved to Cave Creek, a town north of Phoenix, with her first husband shortly after graduation from the U of A. She still lived in the same house, although with a different husband. Claire had been visiting here for twenty-five years. When she first came, Cave Creek was a small western town with a post office, a saloon, a few restaurants and an American Legion Hall, but now the main road bustled with restaurants and shops. You could get a latte here, which Claire considered the line of demarcation between the old west and the new. Once the roads leading into Cave Creek were lined with cactus. But Phoenix and Scottsdale continued to sprawl, and whenever Claire came back she saw more houses. Lynn had bought ten acres when land was cheap. The lay of her land was such that not another house was, or ever would be, visible from hers. The world outside sprawled and spread, but Lynn's property remained the same. The house, which had been built by her first husband, was simple but comfortable. The land and the view were spectacular. Claire believed there were indoor houses and outdoor houses. The Grangers spent most of their time outdoors.

When Claire pulled into the driveway, she saw Lynn and her husband, Steve, in the yard. Lynn wore jeans and a baggy T-shirt. She was letting her hair go gray and her body get plump. Claire hoped this was a sign of contentment. Lynn walked over to the truck followed by Steve, who had thin, sharp features and worried eyes. He had lost weight, which gave him the dry, scrawny look of a desert plant. Lynn looked like a well-tended and nourished house plant. The weight that had fallen off Steve appeared to have settled on her, as if a transfer of power had taken place. Steve had had heart surgery recently and he took it as a wake-up call. He learned how to reduce stress, exercise and watch his diet. Some of the most contented men Claire knew were men who had recovered from heart surgery, but she wasn't sure she would put Steve in that category.

"Good to see you," he said, shaking her hand.

"You, too," Claire replied.

Lynn gave her a hug. "How was the funeral?"

"Difficult."

"You need a glass of Chardonnay," Lynn said.

"You're right."

Steve got the wine and they sat down on the patio. It was the time just before sunset known as civil twilight, Claire's favorite time of day, a reminder that peace and civility were possible. As the sun dropped near the horizon, the shadows of the saguaros lengthened. Their curved arms reached up in a way that made them appear almost human. They sat in silence for a few minutes while the sun dropped behind the horizon, silhouetting the Seven Sisters Mountains against the sky. The mountains here were round and gentle, in contrast to the jagged Sandias behind Claire's house. It was a time of near-perfect stillness. Then the sky darkened, the stars came out and the coyotes began to yip. Steve excused himself to make dinner.

"How was the ex?" Lynn asked as soon as he had disappeared into the house.

"All right, I guess. I didn't talk to him for long."

"And the new wife?"

Claire shrugged. "She was there, but I managed to avoid her. I went back to the sorority house after the funeral."

"Oh, God, what was it like after all this time?"

"I felt like I didn't belong there and maybe I never had. Next I went to see Elizabeth, who was being bitchy to her boyfriend's daughter."

"She always was bitchy, wasn't she? What did you think of Jess? You did meet him, didn't you? I can't imagine Elizabeth not showing her trophy off to everyone who visits."

"Is that how she thinks of him?"

"Most likely," Lynn said.

"He seemed nice."

"Nice? Do you think Elizabeth keeps him around because he's *nice?*"

"All right, he's young, tall, good-looking, but Elizabeth seems to be sapping his energy."

"She does that to everyone, which is why her relationships never last. Once the conquest is over and she has a man totally under her control, she gets bored."

"When I visited the sorority house, I saw a Goodwill box, and it reminded me of the time Elizabeth accused Miranda Kohl of robbing her. Do you remember that?"

"I remember, and I know Miranda was not the thief." Lynn was vehement in her defense, reminding Claire that she and Miranda had kept in touch all these years. Lynn had once wanted to be an actress and lived out her unfulfilled dream by following Miranda's career. Considering that Miranda's career had brought her to the point of posing as an old woman in Lemon Pledge commercials, Claire thought Lynn might have made the wiser choice. She had a devoted husband. She lived in a beautiful place.

"Evelyn was her roommate then. Did you ever consider that she was the thief?" Claire asked.

"Not at the time, but it makes perfect sense now."

Eventually Steve called them in for dinner. As far as Claire could tell nothing but the photographs had changed inside the house in all the years she'd been coming here. The brown sofa in the living room appeared to be the same brown sofa she'd seen on her first visit. Lynn had never been very interested in decorating. They sat down at the table and Steve served a dinner that would have pleased a cardiologist. Claire couldn't find a drop of fat anywhere. The chicken had been grilled and the skin removed. The potatoes were boiled and so was the asparagus. Desert was a dish of strawberries, no cream, no sugar. Lynn couldn't be putting on the pounds eating like this.

She took a few bites, complimented her husband on his cooking, then returned the conversation to Evelyn. "I didn't think of her when the credit card bills appeared, but Steve did."

"I knew the house wasn't robbed," he said, cutting into his chicken. "We're always home. Anyone robbing mailboxes around here would be noticed because there's so little traffic on the road. The other guests we've had were all family or close

82

friends. Why would Evelyn look Lynn up after all this time? I didn't believe her when she said she wanted to move to Cave Creek. It's isolated, it's not a good place for a single woman. I told her she'd be happier in Santa Fe."

"Do you think Evelyn would have been happy anywhere?" Claire asked.

"No," Lynn replied.

"Have you seen Miranda recently?" Claire asked.

"She and her husband, Erwin, live in New River now. She's on location a lot, but we see them when they are in town. Erwin and Steve play golf together."

"You'd enjoy meeting him," Steve said. "He can be entertaining. I could invite him over tomorrow."

"Any excuse to play golf." Lynn laughed.

"He's an actor himself," Steve said. "He's done TV and movies."

"He's not getting much work these days," Lynn said. "So he does his performing in real life."

"I'll call him," Steve said.

Shortly after dinner Claire excused herself and went to bed. She fell asleep immediately but woke up later when moonlight beamed in through her window. She got up to go to the bathroom, following the glow of a nightlight down the dark hallway. On her way back to her room she glanced out the window and saw Lynn sitting alone on the patio hugging a bag of potato chips as if she were clutching a pillow. The moonlight was bright enough that Claire could see her dip her hand into the bag, pull out a chip, put it in her mouth. It was an automatic gesture, as if she was sleep-eating. Late-night eating would explain the weight gain. During the evening she had seemed content to Claire, but something had to be wrong to make her get up in the middle of the night to eat. Claire thought it would be an invasion of Lynn's privacy to interrupt her, so she went back to bed.

When she woke again, it was morning. She dressed and went into the kitchen, where she found her hosts having a break-fast of dry toast and fruit.

"Did you sleep all right?" Lynn asked her.

"Fine. And you?"

"Very well," Lynn said.

The little lies, Claire thought, that grease the engine of friendship. She helped herself to a slice of mango.

"I called Erwin and he's coming over," Steve said. "We'll play some golf and let the two of you talk."

★ ★ ★

Erwin arrived during coffee. From the kitchen window they could see him pull into the driveway. He drove the kind of oversized, overpriced SUV that made Claire think she'd need a tank for protection. The downside of the prosperity of the nineties was that everything — even the people — was getting oversized.

"He's not as bad as he looks. He can be quite funny," Lynn whispered to Claire as Steve let Erwin in.

He was a big man, in girth if not in height, with the kind of straight-backed posture Claire admired, but holding his back straight made his stomach protrude. Claire had the sensation he was the drummer in a marching band and his taut belly was the drum. Playing the part of a golfer, Erwin wore knickers and a navy blue shirt. His hair was slick and black and his complexion ruddy. He wasn't good-looking enough to be a leading man, but he exuded a certain vitality. Claire supposed he could qualify for character parts, although the uniqueness of his looks might limit the number of roles.

"How are you, Erwin?" Lynn asked.

"All the better for seeing you," he replied, kissing her cheek. "And who is your lovely friend?" He turned toward Claire.

"Claire Reynier, Erwin Bush. We were sorority sisters at the U of A."

"Miranda never mentioned you," Erwin replied, taking Claire's hand and holding it longer than seemed necessary. "She doesn't much like to talk about her U of A days. She was treated very shabbily by that sorority, very, very shabbily. But as they say, revenge is a dish best served cold. Past hurts will be forgotten when she stars in her own TV series next fall."

"What's it about?" Claire asked.

"I can't say." He put his index finger to his lips. "Very hush-hush. Miranda is on location in Mexico. She and I communicate by cell phone and e-mail, but I will tell her that I met you. I'm sure she will be delighted. Are you from Arizona?"

"New Mexico. I was in Tucson for the funeral of my former mother-in-law," Claire said.

"Don't forget the death of Evelyn Martin," Lynn added.

"And who is Evelyn Martin?" Erwin asked.

"Another sorority sister who traveled around the Southwest visiting her old friends and stealing from them," Lynn said. "She was once Miranda's roommate. She was found dead in a rental house in Santa Fe. A house that we all paid for. I forgot to

86

ask what else she took from you," she said to Claire. "Detective Amaral told me she stole something personal from each of us."

"She took a signed first edition of Herman Melville's *The Confidence-Man*," Claire said.

"What did Evelyn take from —" she began to ask, but Lynn mouthed the word *later*, leaving Claire feeling that a half-formed sentence was dangling from her lip.

Erwin filled the void. "I once saw an off-Broadway production of *The Confidence-Man*. The show never made it to Broadway. It wasn't a very good script or a very theatrical book. There was no hook. The playwright never got a fix on the character. Personally I don't think Melville ever got a fix on him either."

"It wasn't his best book," Claire agreed.

"My favorite was *Moby-Dick*," Steve said.

"That's everybody's favorite," Lynn said.

"Ready to play some golf?" Steve asked Erwin.

"Ready," Erwin replied.

The men went off to play golf and the women sat on the terrace drinking coffee. Claire had an extra cup to rev herself up for the drive back to Albuquerque.

"Remember the time we were sitting here and a mother quail walked across the driveway with her babies tagging along behind her and the dad bringing up the rear?" Lynn asked.

Claire remembered. One of her joys in visiting Cave Creek was the wildlife. Over the years she had seen a coyote lope down Lynn's driveway, a rattlesnake slither across the floor of the garage, a javelina snort through the garbage, a desert skunk with a plumed tail, numerous quail and several hawks. Wildlife visited Albuquerque, too, but it was rarely visible. At home Claire heard coyotes barking in the foothills, but she had never seen one.

"I belong to a group that protects quail," Lynn said. "I keep them for a few days before they are released back into the wild. I don't have any at the moment, but that's where I keep them." She pointed to a pen on the far side of the driveway. "Last year the group released four hundred quail. Those birds wouldn't have survived without our help."

Lynn was a gentle environmentalist who resembled a quail herself, unlike the hawkish Elizabeth. Claire knew there was room for both types in the environmental movement. Lynn was so proud of the group's accomplishment and her role in it that Claire didn't have the heart to point out that quail were predator fodder. The more quail that survived, the more rattlesnakes and hawks would survive. Nature was full of checks and balances. Claire thought more of all of them would be a good thing, but she didn't have to worry about stepping on a rattlesnake in her garage.

There remained the issue of the unfinished sentence, so she picked up where she had left off earlier. "You didn't tell me what Evelyn took from your house that you valued," she said.

"I didn't want to talk about it in front of Steve," Lynn replied, staring into the desert as if she were hoping some wildlife would come along to divert Claire's attention and change the subject. "I started eating when he was in the hospital; I was so afraid I would lose him. The only thing that made me feel better was eating. Then he survived and came home and now all he can eat is low-fat food. It would be cruel to pig out in front of him. I wake up in the middle of the night scared to death that he'll have another heart attack, and I get up and eat. I can't fit into any of my old clothes. All I can wear are these baggy jeans and T-shirts. I had a couple of caches of food hidden in the garage. Evelyn must have found one and taken it. I know that now, but when I first noticed it was missing I thought Steve might have found it and thrown it away. I didn't dare say anything because I was afraid to reveal I was secretly eating if he didn't already know."

How could he not know? Claire wondered, watching the wings of skin flap under her friend's arms. "Did you tell anybody about the food theft?"

Lynn's eyes searched the desert as she answered. "Only Miranda."

"She knew Evelyn had visited you?"

Lynn nodded.

"Did she suspect Evelyn when you told her the food was missing?"

"She did, but I didn't believe Evelyn would steal from me until Amaral called. He found the box of food in her house. When he described it, I knew it was mine."

"It would have been very easy for Miranda to take the next step and assume that Evelyn had framed her back in college."

Lynn didn't respond.

"Did she?" Claire asked.

"What?" Lynn asked.

"Make the leap that Evelyn had framed her in college?"

"Yes," Lynn admitted.

"Did you know that Evelyn had moved to Santa Fe?"

"Not until Amaral called. Don't tell him about Miranda and Evelyn, Claire. I don't want to make any trouble for her."

"Somebody needs to tell him," Claire said. "Evelyn was murdered. He suspects one of us, but Miranda would have had more of a motive."

"It wasn't Miranda. She wouldn't kill anyone, and I know it wasn't you either," Lynn added, squeezing Claire's hand. "Amaral could be wrong. Maybe it wasn't any of us."

"Maybe," Claire said. "Wouldn't Miranda have told Erwin about the food theft and that Evelyn was here? He just said that he didn't know who Evelyn was."

"I asked her not to tell him. I didn't want Erwin to tell Steve about the food."

Claire, who knew well enough that promises made not to confide in spouses were not always kept, wondered just how good an actor he was.

"It was awful the way Evelyn died." Lynn shivered even though the temperature had already risen above ninety degrees.

"You mean being hit on the head with a blunt object?" Claire asked.

"No. That would have been quick."

"Not necessarily," Claire said. "Maybe she was incapacitated and she lay on the floor until she starved to death or died of dehydration."

"I didn't think of that. What was awful to me was dying all alone and not being missed until the body had decomposed."

"I thought that was just the fear of people who live alone," Claire said.

"It's the fear of everyone," Lynn replied. She shook her baggy T-shirt as if she was shaking crumbs out of her lap and stood up. "Can you stay for lunch?"

"I should get going. It's a long drive, and I have to be at work tomorrow."

Driving up I-17 to Flagstaff, at the point where the road began to gain elevation just north of Black Canyon City, Claire got stuck behind an oversized load with flags on the tail end. It appeared to be a prefabricated house. On its own plot of land, it would be a very small house, but on the road it was an insurmountable obstacle that symbolized the way Claire was beginning to feel about the death of Evelyn Martin. She hadn't intended to be doing Amaral's job when she visited her former classmates in Arizona. She wasn't an investigator. All she'd planned to do was share a bad experience with others who'd had the same experience. But now she had learned something that Amaral probably didn't know, and the question of what to do about it nagged her. Miranda had left school shortly after the theft. Claire had never seen her again except for the TV appearances and commercials that Lynn told her about. All she knew about Miranda now was what she had witnessed on the screen, heard from Lynn and could surmise from meeting Erwin. But Miranda had a motive the other sisters did not. The rest of the women had been wounded and inconvenienced by the thefts, but Miranda had been forced to drop out of school. There must have been a time when she felt embittered by the experience. Although Claire didn't know her anymore, she was reluctant to point the finger at anyone, even if it meant pointing the finger of suspicion away from herself.

As she poked along behind the house, she thought about New River, where Miranda and Erwin lived. In some ways it resembled Cave Creek, but it was farther from Phoenix and less developed. It was tempting to turn around to get out from behind the house. By now there was a half mile of impatient vehicles behind her and she felt squeezed between them and the hard place of the prefab house. But Erwin was playing golf with Steve and Miranda was on location in

Mexico. There was no one to visit in New River, and she remained stuck behind the house until it turned west at Flagstaff.

Claire made good time the rest of the way. There was an hour of daylight left when she got home, time to tend her roses. Nemesis was so glad to be let out of the house that he darted out the door without even acknowledging her return. She checked the messages and found one from her daughter asking about the funeral. Hoping to take advantage of the daylight, she planned to call Robin later. She put on gardening gloves, grabbed a pair of shears and went into her yard. There were ten large rosebushes along the east-facing wall planted by the previous owner of the house. Claire loved the roses, but she wouldn't have planted them herself; they required too much attention and too much water. She felt guilty about pouring so much water on a plant. But since the roses were already there, she was obliged to tend them. They rewarded her in spring with a wall of color. There were three different types of roses on her wall. The Don Juans were a deep, dark red. The Saint Josephs started out yellow then turned orange and red as they opened. The Sweethearts were almost magenta in color. There were places where the branches of one type of rose crisscrossed the branches of another, continually forming new and rich color combinations and reminding Claire that colors in nature never clashed.

She had a drip irrigation system that allowed her to go away in the summer. It was enough to keep the roses alive, but not enough to keep them blooming. The roots required deep and regular watering, which she accomplished by moving a hose from plant to plant and letting it run slowly until the ground was saturated. While she waited for the roses to drink, she cut off spent blossoms, a process known as deadheading.

Claire considered concentrating on the task and the beauty of the blossoms as a form of meditation, a meditation that could be interrupted at any time by the prick of a thorn. It was always a surprise that something so small could cause so much pain, but knowing the thorns were in the roses increased her level of concentration. Claire knew that the solutions to problems were often found by concentrating on something else. When she finished trimming and watering the roses, she cut the best blossom from each plant, took them inside, put them in a vase and filled it with water. While she arranged the flowers, it occurred to her that she should call Miranda, explain her di-

lemma and hope that Miranda would contact Amaral herself. It might be an
unrealistic and naïve hope, but it could re-
lieve Claire of the burden of telling Amaral.

She didn't have Miranda's number, so
she dialed information and learned that the
number was unlisted, which made sense for
an actress. Claire could have gotten the
number from Lynn, but Lynn might want to
talk her out of contacting Miranda. She
asked information if there was a listing for
Erwin Bush and got his number. She supposed having a listed number made some
kind of statement about Erwin's career.

He answered with a gruff "Hello."

"Erwin," she said, "this is Claire Reynier.
I met you this morning at Lynn and Steve
Granger's."

"My pleasure," Erwin replied. "Are you
back in Albuquerque?"

"Yes."

"I hope you had a good drive."

"It was fine, thank you. I'd like to get in
touch with Miranda. Could you tell me how
to reach her?"

"It's hard for Miranda to talk when she is
on location. I would be happy to give her
your number and have her call you. Would
that do?"

"All right," Claire said. "My number is —"

Erwin rattled off the number before she could. "I have caller I.D.," he said.

It didn't surprise her that her number would come up on caller I.D.; it happened all the time. Claire never felt a need to hide who she was from the people she called. She hadn't blocked her name from coming up along with her number. She was surprised that Erwin hadn't used her name when he answered the phone; people usually did once they discovered who was calling.

After she finished talking to Erwin, she called her daughter in Boston. "What did you think of the funeral?" Robin asked.

"It was a lovely funeral, the right funeral for Nana," Claire replied.

"Dad called this morning. He's so sad."

"I'm sure he is."

"He said you were looking well. I believe he misses you, Mom." There was a wistful note in Robin's voice that Claire didn't want to hear.

"Your father has a new wife, Robin. Our marriage is over," Claire said, even though she knew that when there were children involved a marriage was never really over.

Chapter Seven

When Claire got to the center the following morning she called the rare book dealers to see if they had any information about her *Confidence-Man.* No one did. Then she called her friend John Harlan and asked if he could meet her for dinner. John bought and sold rare books for Page One, Too in Albuquerque. A book of the caliber of *The Confidence-Man* wasn't likely to end up in Albuquerque, but it might pass through on its way somewhere else. The fact that it was stolen not far from the store by someone who might not have appreciated its worth could have landed it at Page One, Too. If John had come across an exceptional book on the Southwest, he would have told Claire, but there was no reason for him to tell her about a book by Herman Melville. She had never told him she owned a copy of *The Confidence-Man.* Perhaps she just wanted to talk to him. She had fallen into the habit of discussing her professional problems with him, although not her personal problems. John had known Evan, and Claire had known John's deceased wife, but they rarely talked about either of them.

She left the center early. Traffic was lighter than usual crossing town, and she got to Page One, Too sooner than she expected. She walked through the store, said hello to the people she knew behind the counter and went to the door to John's office. As always, it was a mess. Price guides, papers and books were scattered everywhere. John sat in front of a blank computer screen wearing jeans and a rumpled shirt. She hadn't expected him to be deep in conversation with an attractive woman with auburn hair. Could they be talking about books? Claire wondered. Somehow she didn't think so. She glanced at the clock on the wall, noticed that she was ten minutes early and slipped out of the doorway. Then she didn't know where to go. If she returned to the store, the staff would wonder why she was wandering around by herself. There was a small room between John's inner office and the store where his most valuable books were kept. She checked the shelves to see if there were any Melvilles. There weren't. The most valuable books here were all about the Southwest. She couldn't hear John's conversation, yet she felt as if she were eavesdropping. Not knowing what to do next, she was thinking about leaving when the woman came to the door, flashed a toothy smile and walked out through the store. Claire entered John's office and found him standing up and smiling, too.

"Claire," he said. "I haven't seen you for a while. How have you been?"

"Fine," Claire replied. "And you?"

"Good. Where would you like to go for dinner?"

Claire had eaten enough dinners with John to know that his taste in food ran to barbecue, chicken-fried steak and mashed potatoes. He had been raised in Texas. You could take the man out of Texas, but you couldn't take Texas out of the man. Every time Claire had tried to introduce him to new foods he just picked at them. The one place they had been able to compromise was on Italian food. The prickly part of her wanted to choose a restaurant that she knew he wouldn't like, but she repressed it and suggested Emilios.

"Sounds good," John said.

They walked out to the parking lot and got into their respective vehicles. Emilios was a short drive down Montgomery, long enough for Claire to remind herself that when John had tried to be romantic she had rebuffed him, but not long enough for her to come to the conclusion that he had only been selling books to the woman in his office.

He ordered spaghetti with meat sauce. Claire ordered the most unusual entrée she could find on the menu, spaghetti with clam sauce.

"What have you been up to?" John asked, leaning forward and resting his arms on the table.

"Evan's mother died. I went to Arizona for the funeral."

"That must have been uncomfortable."

"Very."

"Evan's a fool, but I am sorry to hear that his mother died. No matter what kind of dumb mistakes you make in life, your mother's the one who'll understand and forgive you."

It wasn't the relationship Claire had with her own mother, but she let that slide. "Did I ever tell you that I had a signed first edition of Melville's *The Confidence-Man*?"

John shook his head. "I would have remembered if you had. A signed first edition is worth at least eight thousand dollars."

"Ten thousand," said Claire. "My copy was stolen from my house by a former classmate at the U of A. She replaced it with the Oxford World's Classics edition. I didn't notice the substitution until the police told me it had been stolen. There's always a possibility that my first edition will turn up at Page One, Too."

"It's possible, but it's not likely. The people I would try are Tom Butterworth, Simon Collins and Brett Moon. There's a very limited number of buyers for a book of that quality. It'll end up where people have real money, not in Albuquerque."

"I called all of them. No one has seen it."

John leaned back in his chair. "For a bookworm, you sure lead an exciting life."

"It's getting too exciting," Claire said. "The woman who took *Confidence-Man* was found dead in her house in Santa Fe, hit on the head with a blunt object."

"Not a book, I hope. I've seen some that were heavy enough to be a murder weapon."

In spite of herself, Claire laughed. When John was in the right setting, he could be an entertaining companion. "I suspect the weapon had something to do with cooking. The body was found in the kitchen."

"Maybe it was a cookbook."

"Maybe."

The spaghetti arrived and John began twirling his around on his fork. "There are people who would consider a stolen book cause for murder, but I know you well enough to know you wouldn't even consider it."

"Thanks for the vote of confidence," Claire said.

She climbed into bed that night surrounded by her favorite books. The flames in her gas fireplace leapt to life as she clicked the remote. It was getting too warm for a fire and this could be the last one of the season. Watching fire led to speculation and her thought was that the more men a woman let into her life, the more complications she would have. It had been simpler to let one man — her husband — epitomize all men, but when he walked out it left a crater. The foreboding sensation she'd had when she saw John talking to the woman in his office left her feeling that she must still be suffering a hangover from Evan's betrayal, or maybe the wound had been reopened when she saw Evan and Melissa together. She and John had made no commitments to each other. She had liked the ambiguous quality of their relationship. They were friends now. Maybe someday they would be lovers. But how long would John remain interested in a potential love affair if a warm body showed up? Was the woman in his office a warm body? Would a relationship with her end his friendship with Claire? She had no way of knowing, but John hadn't acted any differently at dinner, and she fell asleep wrapped in that comforting thought.

Chapter Eight

Later in the week Claire received a call from the student who manned the information desk saying she had a visitor. The student hadn't gotten the name of the visitor, so she walked out to see who was there and was startled to find Detective Dante Amaral waiting for her.

"Detective Amaral?" she asked. "What are you doing here?"

"Can we talk?" he asked.

"Let's go to the food court and get a cup of coffee," she suggested.

"I'd prefer to talk in your office," he replied. His voice seemed to have gotten more precise since the last time they talked.

Claire didn't want to be seen arguing with him at the information desk so she led him down the hallway to her office. She shut the door behind them, sat down at her desk and offered him the visitor's chair. Amaral remained standing just long enough to remind her how tall he was. She was tempted to close the blinds, but that was sure to arouse the curiosity of her coworkers.

"This is a beautiful building," Amaral said once he sat down. "It must be a pleasure to work here."

"It is," Claire replied.

"Can you tell me where you were on the evening of April twenty-first?" he asked. Clearly the amenities were over.

"Not offhand."

"Would you check your calendar, please?" The words were polite but clipped, the manner less deferential than it had been at their last meeting.

Had he come to her office, Claire wondered, to surprise her? Would he know her calendar was in her office and she wouldn't have time to concoct an alibi with him sitting right in front of her? Had he been able to establish a time of death? Whatever date he mentioned she knew she had done nothing wrong, but he was making her feel that she had. She checked the calendar on her computer and found no entry for the evening of April 21.

She told the truth. "I don't have anything entered. I suppose I was home taking care of my garden or my cat."

"Do you have any witnesses?"

"Not that I recall. Why?"

"We have reason to believe that was the evening Evelyn Martin was murdered. The postmarks on her mail indicated that was the last day she picked it up. A runner on

Tano Road saw two women arguing in front of the house near six-thirty p.m. One of the women fits your description."

Six-thirty would have given Claire plenty of time to get to Tano Road after work. "I didn't go to Santa Fe that evening," she said. "If I had it would be entered on my calendar."

Amaral's quizzical expression implied it would be easy enough to delete an entry from a computer calendar. Claire thought he was underestimating her intelligence. If she had wanted to conceal her whereabouts, she would have entered something else on that date. Something in the runner's description made Amaral consider her a suspect. Was this the time when she was supposed to hire a lawyer? But hiring a lawyer seemed to imply she had done something wrong and she knew she had done nothing wrong.

"What exactly was the runner's description?" she asked.

"I can't reveal that information," was his tight-lipped response.

It seemed to be time to tell him about Miranda, although Claire regretted that the job had fallen to her.

"There's something else you need to know," she said. "A woman in our sorority

106

named Miranda Kohl was Evelyn Martin's roommate. Elizabeth Best came across Miranda wearing her jacket and caused an unpleasant scene. The housemother investigated and found Miranda's closet full of stolen clothes. Miranda was forced to leave the sorority house. She dropped out of school and became an actress." Claire hated to bring up Lynn's name, but she felt she must. "Lynn Granger has stayed in touch with Miranda over the years. She told her Evelyn had visited and had most likely robbed her. It wouldn't have been hard for Miranda to make the deduction that Evelyn Martin had been the one who stole the clothes and framed her in college."

"How would this Miranda Kohl have known that Evelyn Martin was in Santa Fe?"

Because Lynn's husband suggested she move there? Claire wondered, but her response was, "How would any of us have known?"

Amaral shrugged. "How long have you known about Miranda Kohl?"

"I knew about the theft in college, but I had forgotten about it until I went back to Arizona last weekend and visited the sorority house. I saw Lynn on Sunday and she said Miranda had told her she believed Evelyn had robbed her."

"Can you tell me how to reach this Miranda?"

"She's on location for a TV show, but her husband can connect you."

While Claire looked up the number and wrote it down, Amaral's eyes circled her office taking in the books on her shelves. Harrison walked by the window. His eyes landed and lingered on Detective Amaral. Claire wondered if he could tell that she was talking to a detective. The thought made her feel guilty, although she knew she had nothing to be guilty about. She knew that even to think of guilt could make it appear on one's face, and she feared that Detective Amaral would read it in her expression.

"Have you been able to locate *The Confidence-Man*?" he asked.

"No," she said. "None of the dealers I contacted have seen it. Are you sure it wasn't at Evelyn's? Did you search the house thoroughly?"

"Very thoroughly. The book was not there." Amaral's lips tightened, suggesting he didn't enjoy being questioned himself. He changed the subject. "I'd like the dealers' names and addresses," he said.

Claire wrote them down for him.

After he left she reflected that although none of the sisters had admitted to knowing that Evelyn was living in Santa Fe, it was possible that one or more of them had known. Evelyn might have told Elizabeth or Jess where she was living. Ginny might have run into her somewhere. Evelyn might even have told Lynn, although Claire didn't like to think Lynn would conceal that fact from her. She wondered whether Evelyn had made it into the Santa Fe phone book. She got on the Internet, searched the Santa Fe White Pages and found the phone number and address listed on Tano Road. All it took was knowing, or suspecting, that she lived in Santa Fe to locate her.

When Harrison came back later in the day, Claire wasn't surprised to see him. He picked up a glass paperweight from her desk, balanced it in his long white fingers and paused before he spoke. She supposed he was debating how to ask whom she had been talking to, but she didn't intend to give him any help.

"You were talking to a detective earlier?" he asked.

It must have been the graduate student at the information desk, Claire thought. He heard her say "Detective Amaral" and told Harrison. She'd have a word later with that student. "Yes," she admitted.

"Have we had another theft?" Harrison asked. It wasn't so long ago that a valuable box of books had been stolen from Claire's truck.

"*We* haven't, but I have," she replied. "I had a signed first edition of Herman Melville's *The Confidence-Man* stolen from my bedroom by a friend from my college days who visited me last year. The woman was found dead in her house in Santa Fe along with a list of stolen property. I didn't notice the book was missing until the detective told me." Claire didn't say that the detective believed Evelyn Martin had been murdered and that she herself was a suspect. "The man you saw in my office, Detective Dante Amaral from the Santa Fe Police Department, is investigating the theft."

"That's a valuable book to be sure. Melville signed a very limited number of copies."

"I'm aware of that. I called the rare book dealers who were likely to come across it, but no one has yet."

Harrison stared at the paperweight as if he were looking into a crystal ball. "I did my dissertation on Herman Melville."

"So I heard."

"*The Confidence-Man* was the last book Melville published in his lifetime."

Harrison had a knack for telling Claire things she already knew.

"It was too metaphysical, too full of the existential enigma of the self to ever be a popular book," Harrison said.

Claire had the sense she had heard that phrase before. It was possible Harrison had used it in another context. This was a man who punctuated his sentences with "to be sure."

"I didn't know you collected Melville," Harrison said.

"I don't," Claire replied. "That book was offered to me when I worked at the U of A library, and I bought it."

"It's the one book of his I don't have in a first edition."

"Oh?" Claire responded.

"Signed first editions are very rare. You'll be sure to let me know, won't you, if you get it back?" Harrison put the paperweight down on her desk with a thump.

"All right," Claire said, knowing she had no choice, suspecting that Harrison would want to buy the book from her and would offer her less than it was worth. He was known for his parsimony.

Becoming a murder suspect and having a boss who talked about the existential enigma of the self and coveted a book that rightfully belonged to her was a lot to process in one day. When Claire got home to her house in the foothills, she let Nemesis out, put on a pair of gardening gloves, picked up the pruning shears and went to her wall of roses. The flowers were a kaleidoscope of color — orange, gold, magenta, Don Juan red. Whatever arrangement they formed, they were magnificent. She began cutting off the spent blossoms while she tried to make sense of her day. That Harrison was a pompous pain was a given. That she had to get along with him was also a given. She worked her way through the Sweethearts. That she had become a suspect in a murder investigation was a thought as alien and shocking as discovering a husband had been unfaithful. She had the same sensation she had when she learned about Melissa — could this possibly be happening to her? Could a detective who was young enough to be her son doubt her word? She nipped off a dead magenta flower. She could see how under the pressure of being misunderstood a person might do something totally rebellious and out of character. Perhaps that was what had motivated Evelyn Martin. Had anybody ever understood Evelyn? She began deadheading the

Don Juans. Where would this all lead? She couldn't possibly be arrested or prosecuted for murder, could she? As she reached for a spent blossom a thorn stabbed her arm, drawing blood. The shears clattered as they fell to the ground.

"Goddamn you, Evelyn Martin," she said.

Chapter Nine

Claire spent the weekend indoors; the wicked winds and swirling dust made it unpleasant to be outside. When she wasn't practicing tai chi, she wondered whether she ought to consult a lawyer. There was a woman lawyer in town she knew and liked, but hiring a lawyer lent credence to rumor, gave substance to shadow. If she kept quiet and did nothing, suspicion might blow away. While New Mexico appeared to be drifting past her window on the spring wind, it was easier to believe that what seemed threatening now would be gone tomorrow.

On Monday evening Ginny called her. "Has Dante been in touch with you?" she asked.

"Yes."

"And where were *you* on the evening of April twenty-first, Clairier?" she asked.

"At home. And you?"

"I went out to dinner."

"Are you still finding Dante attractive at this point?"

"He's getting more tense," Ginny said. "Tension can spoil a man's looks."

"I imagine he told you about the runner."

"He did."

"Did he give you any details of the runner's description?"

"No."

"I have to be in Santa Fe on Thursday to look at some books for the library. Would you like to have lunch?"

"I'd love it," Ginny said.

"Could we meet at Geronimo at one?"

"I'll be there."

Claire got to the restaurant first and was sitting at the table when Ginny arrived. She watched her maneuver her way around the tables that filled the room. Her total concentration on the task made it appear that Ginny had already been drinking. Claire wondered if the runner on Tano Road could possibly have mistaken her for Ginny. They both had hair that appeared blond in some lights and gray in others. Claire's hair color was natural. Ginny's wasn't, but that wouldn't make any difference to a casual observer. Ginny was shorter and heavier, but how well could a runner judge height and weight at dusk in a place where the land sloped and the house was hidden by juniper bushes?

"Clairier!" Ginny said when she finally reached the table.

"Hello, Ginny."

"Could we sit outside on the porch?" Ginny pleaded; she could smoke on the porch.

"It's too windy," Claire replied.

"I hate these spring winds. It feels like the air is full of galloping ghosts. Waiter," Ginny called. "A glass of Chardonnay, por favor." She looked at Claire's glass. "And what is that you're drinking?"

"Ginger ale."

"You are so good. You were always so good. It must drive you crazy to be a suspect in a murder investigation."

"I'm not thrilled about it."

"If you wanted to do it you could pull it off, but me . . . Do you believe that anyone would seriously suspect me? When Dante asked where I was on the night of April twenty-first, I had to laugh. I drink. I write artbabble for CultureVulture. I'm everything I pretend to be, but a murderess? I'd never be capable of that. Ah, here comes my Chardonnay. Thank you so very much," she said to the waiter. She turned back to Claire and smiled. "Besides, I have the perfect alibi."

"Oh?"

"I had dinner that night with Miss Lizzie."

"You and Elizabeth had dinner the night

Evelyn Martin was presumed murdered?" Her perfect alibi was far too perfect in Claire's opinion.

"Yup. She was in town for an environmental conference — save the wolves or the whales or the spotted owls. One of those things. She looked me up."

"You didn't tell me you had seen Elizabeth."

"I must have been having a senior moment. It wasn't my idea of a fun way to spend the evening. Lizzie is such a perfect PC princess. She brings out the worst in me. I told her that Forest Watch — the environmental organization she belongs to — is a bunch of smug, arrogant, self-serving trust-fund hippies. I said if anyone found a wolf on private land, that person ought to shoot, shovel and shut up. Lizzie got pissed off and told me I was an ignorant right-wing redneck bitch. 'Proud of it, too,' I told her. I doubt *we'll* ever be having dinner again."

"I saw Elizabeth in Tucson," Claire said. "She didn't tell me she had been in Santa Fe in April or that she had seen you."

"Under the circumstances, would you have told anyone you'd been in Santa Fe in April? She comes here a lot actually for Forest Watch events. I told Dante all about our little dinner."

"Elizabeth implied that whenever Evelyn was murdered her significant other, Jess, would provide her with an alibi."

"He may have been here, too. I ran into Lizzie downtown the next day with a hunk. She had a glow that could have been postcoital, or maybe she's on hormone replacement therapy. I asked her if she was taking Premarin and she said she wouldn't because it wasn't natural. I said horse urine is natural, isn't it? That's what Premarin comes from, you know."

"I know. Where did you and Elizabeth have dinner?"

"Santa Café."

"Did Dante ask for a receipt?"

"Yes, but I didn't have one. Lizzie paid."

"That sounds like a shaky alibi to me," Claire said.

"A lot better than yours, though, isn't it?" Continuing her assault on political correctness, Ginny ordered veal and another glass of wine, although she had yet to finish the first one. Claire ordered the rack of lamb with rosemary.

"Did you say you were in Tucson?" Ginny asked.

"Yes."

"What were you doing there?"

"My ex-husband's mother died and I

went to the funeral."

"That must have been fun."

"Before I went to see Elizabeth I stopped at the sorority house."

"Does it look any better?"

"Somewhat. I saw the Goodwill box and it reminded me of the time Elizabeth came across Miranda Kohl wearing her jacket. Do you remember that?"

"How could I forget? It was one of Lizzie's finest moments." She reached across the table and wagged her finger in Claire's face, doing a sloppy imitation of an angry Elizabeth Best. " 'Take my jacket off right now, bitch, or I'll call the police.' Elizabeth has always suffered from poor anger management. Usually you see more self-control in a PC princess."

In essence it was the incident Claire remembered, although the details differed. She was unable to remember Elizabeth's exact words. She certainly didn't remember the use of the *b* word. "Do you remember who Miranda's roommate was at the time?"

"It was Annie Hutchinson, no?"

"No. It was Evelyn Martin."

"Are you sure?" Ginny's finger paused in midair as she asked this question.

"Yes."

Ginny smiled, and Claire noticed that her

teeth were stained from smoking. She dropped her hand back into her lap. "That's good for you, isn't it?" Ginny asked. "Miranda has a better motive than any of us. So Evelyn was a klepto back then. She robs us, stuffs the clothes in Miranda's closet. Miranda gets blamed. Years later she finds out that Evelyn has robbed again. She goes to see her to settle up the old score. Evelyn feels threatened when Miranda confronts her. She attacks. Miranda fights back and bops her over the head. . . . Only how did Miranda find out that Evelyn had robbed again?"

"Lynn told her that Evelyn had visited and something she valued had disappeared."

"They always were good friends, weren't they? What has become of Miranda anyway?"

"She's an actress. She's shooting a new TV series in Mexico."

"Did you tell Dante about Evelyn and Miranda being roommates and all?"

"I felt that I had to."

"Of course you did," Ginny soothed. "We have to do whatever it takes to protect ourselves. They don't serve veal and Chardonnay in the state pen."

When the veal arrived, Ginny ordered another glass of Chardonnay. By the time the meal was over she had four wineglasses in varying degrees of fullness lined up in front of her as if she was a pack rat stockpiling sustenance for a dry day. Would those glasses be considered half full or half empty? Claire wondered. When the check arrived, the waiter placed it in the middle of the table. Ginny grabbed for it.

"I'll get it," Claire said.

"It's on me," Ginny replied, whipping out her credit card.

"It was my idea to have lunch."

"Don't worry about it. I had an excellent divorce lawyer."

As they left the restaurant, Ginny wove her way through the maze of tables, bumping into one and apologizing for the silverware that clattered to the floor.

When they reached the parking lot, Claire became afraid to send Ginny out onto the road in her condition. Even if she didn't hurt herself, she could hurt someone else. She lived close enough that she could walk home, but Claire doubted she would.

"I'd be happy to give you a ride home," she offered. "You could take a nap, walk back, pick up your car later."

"What do I need a nap for?" Ginny snapped.

"You've been drinking."

"I had one glass of wine. Big deal. So what?"

"You had four glasses of wine."

"I did not."

"You did. I counted them."

"You're counting my drinks, Clairier?" Ginny's face turned red and puffy with anger. Like liquid in a too-full glass her emotions seemed to be sloshing over the edge. "Who the hell are you? My mother?"

Claire put out her hand. "Just give me the keys, Ginny."

"You know ever since you reappeared in my life, you've done nothing but criticize me. I write artbabble. I drink too much. I lied about my alibi. Well you're wrong about one thing. I'm quite capable of driving my own self home if you would just get the fuck out of my way." She took the keys from her purse and shook them in Claire's face.

A well-dressed woman walking down Canyon Road stopped and stared at them. A tussle in Geronimo's parking lot went beyond unseemly in Claire's mind. She stepped aside, let Ginny pass and watched her stumble across the parking lot to her car, wondering what to do next. About the only thing she could do now was follow her home, and then what? Pick up the pieces if Ginny ran into something on the way? As Claire began walking toward her truck, she heard the sounds of an engine starting and wheels crunching gravel. Then the sound of a car racing across the lot. Claire turned around to see Ginny's black BMW backing rapidly in her direction.

"Stop," she yelled, but Ginny seemed to have lost control of the car and it careened toward Claire.

Time entered another dimension. The BMW was speeding toward Claire, yet at the same time it appeared to be moving in slow motion, allowing her time to watch in disbelief. She knew she had to get out of its path. She needed shelter and she needed protection. The only shelter handy was under the bed of her truck. At the last second Claire threw herself out of the way and under the truck. Ginny hit the brake and the car spun gravel, barely missing the next vehicle. The gravel flew like buckshot and stung Claire. She felt she was a shooting-gallery target that had been shot full of holes. Ginny shut off her engine, opened the door, jumped out and ran toward Claire, who was crawling out from under her truck.

"Oh, God," she cried. "I must have popped it into reverse instead of drive. I am so very sorry, Clairier."

Claire brushed the gravel from her hands and knees and examined herself, half expecting to find bullet holes but seeing only scrapes and bruises. "You don't need to floor your car to get out of the parking lot, Ginny."

"Sorry," she mumbled, letting her shoulders droop. Her spine appeared to contract as her body sank into a posture of remorse. She handed Claire the keys. "Would you park my car and give me a ride home in your truck, please?"

Claire took the keys and got into Ginny's car, which was still in reverse. She looked at the gears and saw that one would have to be very out of control or very drunk to mistake reverse for drive.

Ginny huddled in the corner of Claire's cab and her body language was contrite on the way home. All she said was, "When I knew you in college, I never would have imagined you driving a truck."

Ginny apologized again when they reached her house. Claire gave her back the car keys and said, "Promise me you won't go after your car until you're sober."

"I promise," Ginny replied. "Thanks ever so much for bringing me home."

Claire drove down Acequia Madre and

parked in the first lot she came to, which was at Downtown Subscription, feeling bruised and shaken and not up to driving any farther. Books of the West, the bookstore she intended to visit, was on the far side of town, but the walk would do her good. She walked down Paseo de Peralta past the Gerald Peters Gallery, turned left onto East De Vargas, walked through downtown and across the Plaza. Santa Fe might have been a ghost town for all she saw of it.

All she could think about was Ginny Bogardus, wondering if she had really been angry, drunk and out of control or if she'd been pretending. There was a lot of wine left in the glasses. If she hadn't been drunk, what could have prompted her to aim her car at Claire? Poor anger management, or was Ginny more calculating than she pretended to be? What good would it do her to run over Claire and have two old friends dead in the space of a month? Scaring her, however, might serve some purpose. Obviously she and Elizabeth were not simpatico, but the dinner alibi had served both of their interests. Claire didn't believe it for a minute, but she didn't know what she could do about it other than tell Detective Amaral. She wasn't afraid to tell him, but she hated to think that her only defense was to keep pointing her finger at someone else.

When she got to Books of the West, Josh Brainard sat her down in the back room and left her alone while she picked through a box of Western Americana he had recently acquired from an estate. The routine of picking up the books, examining them and setting aside the ones she thought the library could use helped calm her nerves and restore some sense of tranquility to the day. She found five books she wanted and paid Josh for them.

As she walked out of the store, she glanced at her watch. It was five-thirty. If she left Santa Fe at this hour, she'd be battling commuter traffic as well as driving into the setting sun. There was something else she could accomplish here before she left for home.

With the books in hand, she walked to the main library on Washington, where the bulletin board was always a good source of information. She searched through the notices of lectures, conferences, events, massage therapists, yoga instructors and astrologers and found a posting for Forest Watch on a sheet of recycled construction paper. The notice had a listing of conferences for the spring season. She checked the dates and found there had been a conference in Santa Fe the week of April 21, and the subject had been restoring endangered species to New Mexico's forests. A Web site was listed and a number to call for further information. She copied the URL and phone number.

Then she walked back across town to her truck and drove to Tano Road. The hour of the day when the runner had seen someone arguing with Evelyn Martin was approaching. Claire was curious about the evening light, the lay of the land and how much the runner would have been able to see. As she drove west on Tano Road the sun outlined the clouds with gold and highlighted the dead bug smears on her windshield. At this time of day beauty was intensified, but so was ugliness. It was a light that emphasized every flaw and wrinkle.

Claire remembered exactly where Evelyn's house was and parked in the driveway. Apparently no one had decided to exorcise Evelyn's spirit yet; the house looked just as empty as it had the last time. The windows were still blank. It was a house where someone had died, but Claire had to wonder whether it was a house where someone had lived. Had Evelyn had any life here? She walked down Tano Road and stopped beside the juniper bushes. The land sloped and there were steps leading down toward the house, which would make it possible for two people to stand on different levels and create an illusion about their respective heights. Two people of different sizes might appear to be the same height, or conversely, two people of the same size could appear to be different heights. As the sun sank over the horizon, one last ray moved across Tano Road, warming the stucco walls of the house and landing on Claire's hair. She could see her reflection in one of the blank windows. It was impossible to tell in this light whether her hair was silver or gold. The sun dropped behind the horizon, turning Claire's hair gray and the house the color of mud.

She heard the sound of feet pounding the road and stepped out from behind a juniper. The runner approaching was a thin woman with long white arms and legs and a lanky, loose way of moving. Her light-brown hair bobbed up and down behind her. Claire judged her age to be mid-thirties. She seemed very focused on the run and didn't notice Claire standing in the shadows beside the road.

"Excuse me," Claire said.

The woman darted to the side, then began running in place. "You startled me." She grimaced. "I don't like this house. A woman was murdered here. You're not thinking about renting it, are you?"

"No. I knew Evelyn Martin, the woman who was murdered here."

"Really?" said the woman. She stopped running and stared wide-eyed at Claire.

"Have we ever met?" Claire asked. "You look familiar."

The woman shook her head and said, "I don't believe so."

"Are you the runner who talked to Detective Amaral?"

The woman's hands were on her hips and her knees were slightly bent. Her expression turned wary. "How do you know about that?"

"He thinks it was me you saw arguing with Evelyn Martin." Claire was aware that she was taking a risk. If the woman perceived her as a threat, she might tell Detective Amaral, who could consider this trying to influence a witness. If Amaral indicted her and the case ever went to court, the woman might identify her just because Claire's face had become familiar. If she antagonized the woman, she might identify her because she disliked her.

"It might have been you," the woman said, studying Claire. "It was at this time of day. The sun was setting. The women both had highlighted hair. Their age was around fifty. One of the women was heavier than you."

"How much heavier?"

"One was a fourteen, the other was a twelve, is what I told Amaral."

"What about height?"

"They were about the same height."

"Were they standing on the steps?"

"They might have been."

"Were they arguing?"

"I'm not sure I should be telling you this if Amaral considers you a suspect." She began jogging in place again.

"If I am a suspect, it will come out sooner or later."

"One woman seemed very angry. I heard her call the other one a bitch."

"Had you ever seen Evelyn Martin before then?"

"No — she was reclusive. She never came out of the house. I wish they'd get this place rented and someone would move in. It gives me the creeps."

"Do you live nearby?"

"Just down the road." She looked at her watch. "Is that all?"

"Yes. Thanks for your help."

"Don't mention it."

Claire watched her run away and disappear into the growing darkness like Alice's white rabbit. She looked back at the house and saw the shadows of the juniper reaching for it like arms full of evil intent. The shadows could work on her behalf. She wasn't a lawyer, but she thought a good one could make use of the shadows. The runner was right — this was a spooky place. She got in her car and drove back to Albuquerque.

Chapter Ten

When Claire opened the door to her house that night, she had the same sensation she'd had since learning about Evelyn's death — that her home was not the haven it had once appeared to be. As if he sensed her unease, Nemesis allowed her to pick him up and hug him before darting out the door. She walked through the house, looking for signs of disturbance, wondering if Evelyn Martin had taken anything else while she was here, something that might not have been missed yet. Claire examined the living room, the bedrooms, the bathrooms and the kitchen but found nothing amiss. The mug with coffee residue at the bottom was still in her kitchen sink, an unread newspaper lay on the sofa in the living room, the books in the bedroom were in place on the shelves. She played back the phone messages, found one from Lynn Granger and called her back.

"Did Amaral check your alibi?" Lynn asked.

"Yes."

"I figured if he called me then he contacted all of us. Steve and I were home on April twenty-first. Amaral got in touch with

Miranda and asked her for an alibi, too. She was in Mexico on location for her new show."

"You've heard from Miranda?"

"She contacted me after she heard from Amaral." Lynn paused then asked in a hesitant voice, "How did Amaral know about the connection between Miranda and Evelyn, Claire? Did you tell him?"

"Yes," Claire admitted. "I felt that I had to. I thought she should tell him herself, and I left a message for her with Erwin. But she never called me back. Amaral believes I fit the description of the woman the runner saw arguing with Evelyn."

"Did you tell him about Miranda because you don't have an alibi yourself?"

Although Lynn was speaking, Claire heard Steve's skeptical voice. Lynn was her oldest friend, and Claire had always known her to be a trusting person. She had to overcome some skepticism herself before she told Lynn the truth about her lack of an alibi, but she did it for the sake of honesty and friendship. "Yes," she said. "I was home with my cat as my witness."

"What about Ginny and Elizabeth? Do you know if they have alibis?"

"I had lunch with Ginny today. She told me Elizabeth was in Santa Fe on the night in question and they had dinner together. It sounded like a manufactured alibi to me. After lunch I told her I thought she'd had too much to drink and that she shouldn't drive home. We had an argument, and she almost ran me over with her car."

"Deliberately?"

"I'm not sure whether or not it was deliberate. Maybe she was drunk. Maybe she was pretending to be drunk. It's hard to tell with Ginny." Claire was aware of the Freudian theory that the results of a person's actions could be interpreted as the intent of that person's actions. When the person wasn't willing to admit her motives consciously, the subconscious took over. She supposed that principle could be applied to drinkers. Alcohol made it possible for unacknowledged anger to seize the moment.

"That makes you the only suspect who doesn't have an alibi?" Lynn asked.

"Apparently."

"Amaral can't be serious about suspecting you, Claire, even if you don't have an alibi."

"I hope you're right. I went to Evelyn's house this evening. Amaral's witness ran by and I talked to her. Her description was vague enough to fit any of us. The woman she saw had blond or gray hair and was middle-aged. I suppose Miranda is blonde by now, too."

"The last time I saw her she had red hair. I have it on video. Would you like me to send you a copy?"

"Please."

"The Lemon Pledge commercial and some other clips are on the tape. Have you checked your e-mail today?"

"Not yet."

"Miranda said she was going to send you one."

When Claire got off the phone she got on her computer and found the e-mail from Miranda. "Hi, Claire," it began.

Erwin said you wanted to get in touch with me. It has been a long time, hasn't it? I hope you're doing well. As for me, the new series that I am working on is very promising. I play a mother, wouldn't you know? We're on location in Mexico and I am muy busy. I hardly have a moment to myself. Erwin said you wanted to talk about Evelyn. I did wonder if she had set me up in college, but I didn't believe she was capable of it until recent events. I don't hold a grudge. Time wounds all heels. I have Erwin and my career. My life has turned out well and hers did not. Living well is the best revenge. Hope to see you again one of these days.

Cheers, your old friend,
Miranda Kohl.

Claire supposed that any day now technology would advance to the point where people could affix their signatures to their e-mail, but it hadn't happened yet. Signatures played an important role in Claire's profession. She studied them and felt they could reveal something about the state of mind of the inscriber. She had to rely on the tone of the e-mail to judge Miranda's state of mind. It was so offhand and breezy it might have been dashed off by a college student. Miranda seemed far less troubled about Evelyn Martin than Claire was, but she had been on location on the night in question. She was not a suspect.

Claire began to ache from the tension of the day and from tumbling beneath her truck. She filled her bathtub with hot water, scented it with lavender oil and climbed in. The smell of the lavender and the heat of the water helped to put the day in perspective. The bad news was that Ginny had almost run her over and she had the scrapes and bruises to prove it. From the point of view of the investigation, however, there had been some good news. Elizabeth and Ginny's alibis could well be bogus. The runner had not recognized her, making Amaral's case more circumstantial. That she could be a suspect seemed so absurd — she hoped Amaral would drop his investigation and she would never have to mention the fact that she'd talked to the runner or that she doubted Ginny and Elizabeth's alibis. She revised her getting-divorced mantra and repeated it to herself. "You know who you are, you know what you haven't done."

In the morning she answered Miranda's e-mail. "Nice to hear from you," she wrote. "I'm glad to know you are doing well. I hope our paths cross again someday. I'll look forward to the new series. Your old friend, Claire."

Even though it was a short message, she rewrote it several times before sending it into cyberspace. No matter how often she rewrote it, the college-girl tone remained. It seemed to come naturally for former acquaintances to lapse into the lingo of the time they knew each other. Every group had its own way of talking. These days as people moved in and out of marriages, homes and jobs, language changed to fit their new circumstances. The only person she knew whose language was unlikely to have changed was Harrison. She imagined that the first words he ever spoke were pompous. She thought about his phrase, "the existential enigma of the self." It was one of those phrases that could mean everything or nothing. One possible meaning was that it was the condition of humans to change, redefine themselves and wonder exactly who they were. Her old friends might not be wondering about their own identities, but she was. Even if they weren't lying outright they could be using language to conceal their actions and intent. Miranda's offhand breeziness, Lynn's thoughtful hesitancy, Ginny's drunken bravado, Elizabeth's dramatic anger could all be performances.

It occurred to Claire that Ginny's word didn't have to be the last word about the dinner with Elizabeth. She found the Forest Watch URL and typed it into her computer. The Web site came up. The board members were shown, including Elizabeth Best. Claire couldn't disagree with Ginny's assessment that they all looked like they had benefited from trust funds. For someone whose wineglass was always half full, Ginny was capable of acute observations. The man who ran the organization was named Brian Duval. There was a photograph of him and the rest of the staff, all of whom seemed to be young, good-looking and athletic. Forest Watch had a workshop coming up in Albuquerque on the spotted owl, and Elizabeth Best would be leading that workshop.

Claire looked up her number and called. "Has Detective Amaral been in touch with you about the night of April twenty-first?" she asked.

"Yes. I told him I was in Santa Fe that night having dinner at Santa Café with Ginny. I have the credit card receipt to prove it."

"I had lunch with Ginny yesterday."

"Was she sober?"

"She didn't appear to be. She told me you're involved in the Forest Watch endangered-species program."

"Didn't I tell you that myself?"

"Not that I recall."

"When I talk to Ginny about Forest Watch, she makes rednecked remarks like the only good wolf is a dead one."

"She enjoys ticking you off."

"So I've noticed."

"I read that you're leading a workshop in Albuquerque on the spotted owl."

"I am. Next week."

"Is it open to the public?"

"Yes."

"I'd like to come if that's all right with you."

"Why wouldn't it be?" Elizabeth asked.

"Could we meet for dinner afterward?"

"I don't know if I'll have time for dinner, but you're welcome to come to the workshop. Let's have a drink anyway."

"Do you need a place to stay when you're in town?"

"No. I'll be staying at the Hyatt where the workshop is taking place."

When Lynn's video of Miranda Kohl arrived, Claire made a bowl of popcorn and played it on her VCR. One of the pleasures of being single was that she could eat popcorn and watch videos whenever she wanted to. This one began with the Lemon Pledge commercial. An old woman in a faded dress slowly polished her furniture. She wore her white hair in a topknot and had the shuffling movements that came with osteoporosis and advanced age.

"Let me help you with that, Grandma," said a sweet little girl in a party dress.

"I've always used Lemon Pledge," the grandma said.

"That's why your furniture is so beautiful," the little girl said, smiling at her reflection in a highly polished table. "I can see my face in it."

The commercial was as saccharine as overly sweetened tea. Claire played it several times, hitting the pause button whenever Miranda faced the camera. In the old woman's face she still saw something of the wide-eyed ingenue she had known.

She watched the rest of the video. Most of the segments were bit parts in TV series. In one Miranda played a mother. In another she played a hard-edged businesswoman in a power suit. Claire supposed those were the two roles that were available for actresses in their fifties. As the mother, Miranda's hair was russet-colored and curly. The businesswoman's was slick and black. Claire thought she was more successful as the mother than the businesswoman. Miranda's ingenuous quality didn't serve her well when she played hard-edged. Elizabeth had called her a space case and the Miranda Claire remembered had been a rather vague and dreamy person. When Elizabeth had confronted her, she hadn't fought back. She dropped out of school rather than stand up for her innocence, yet she'd had the spunk to go after parts. Perhaps because she could play a role

141

and didn't have to be herself. It was easy enough to assume an actress wasn't what she pretended to be, but most likely the sentiments expressed in her e-mail were honest. Her life *had* turned out better than Evelyn's. Lynn continued to be proud of their friendship and to follow her career with interest. She thought Miranda lived a more exciting and expressive life than she did, but if Miranda's life was so satisfying, how to explain Erwin Bush? To be fair, Claire had remained married to Evan for twenty-eight years, and she'd always have trouble explaining that.

She remembered that somewhere in her house she had a photo album full of sorority pictures. She searched through bureau drawers and closets until she found it buried on the floor of the guest-room closet beneath a box of family photos. It was a U of A photo album with a photomontage of the campus on the cover. Claire opened the album and came across photographs of Evan when they first started dating in her junior year after she got back from a semester in Europe. A window that opened on her life in Europe closed once she met him. He looked serious and preppy then and he looked serious and preppy now, although with more stomach and less hair. But Claire liked to think that she had changed.

She found a class photo from junior year when all the sisters whose lives had recently intertwined lived in the same corridor on the third floor. Except for Evelyn they all looked surprisingly fresh and prettier than she had remembered. As she recalled, all had boyfriends then except for Evelyn. Had they been cruel to her without being aware of it? Had rejection by the boss in Denver triggered some unhappy memory of an earlier rejection?

Looking beyond the sixties clothes and hairdos, Claire stared into the faces seeking some indicator of what they had become. The firmness of Elizabeth's chin indicated she was already accustomed to getting her own way. Ginny was the perpetual little sister with short hair who tagged along behind the boys. Claire remembered her as being athletic. Somehow her positive energy had turned sour and she had become a woman who drank too much. Lynn had a sunny smile, but Claire knew the darkness behind the sun. Until she met Steve, she had been filling the void with some very worthless men. In this photograph Miranda's theatricality was apparent. Her hair was dark and curly and she wore it in a tangled hippie mop. A long scarf was tossed casually over her shoulder. Claire studied her own picture and found her smile to be more confident than she remembered. She always considered herself a late bloomer. It took a while to grow into her bone structure and discover her personality and her looks. Much of the transformation took place while she was traveling around Europe with Pietro Antonelli. As her mother told her after she came back, "You were a sweet child, but you're much more interesting now."

Evelyn was in the center of the group, a plain, overweight lump even then, a woman men were not likely to notice. She looked older than the other sisters, possibly because she was the only one who wasn't smiling. When had a not-wanting-to-please attitude turned into a wanting-to-harm attitude? Claire wondered. Would anyone have thought then that she was a thief or that someone else in the photo could turn out to be a murderer? When this picture was taken, Evelyn might already have been robbing her friends. Could theft have become an addictive behavior, a drug that she turned to in times of stress?

Chapter Eleven

Claire heard no more from Detective Amaral and fell into the routine of dealing with books and avoiding Harrison Hough at work, of doing tai chi and tending to her rose garden at home, hoping the detective's investigation had taken him elsewhere.

She went to Elizabeth Best's presentation on the spotted owl, which was held in an upstairs conference room at the Hyatt Regency. Claire liked the Hyatt; it had an elegance that was uncharacteristic of Albuquerque and reminiscent of Arizona. Elizabeth was late so Claire had time to study the rest of the people in the room. It was a large room and was nearly full, not surprising since people in New Mexico had strong opinions about preservation of the spotted owl. The people in this room — younger environmental activists as well as older birders — were on the preservation side.

Just at the point when the audience began to get restless, Elizabeth swept into the room followed by a man Claire recognized as the Brian Duval she'd seen on the Web site. The center of a whirlwind with a man in her orbit was exactly where Elizabeth liked to be. While Brian took the mike and introduced Elizabeth as "one of the foremost environmentalists in the Southwest," Claire wondered whether Ginny would classify him as a hunk. He had the height and the curly blond hair but wore the narrow, thick-rimmed glasses of an intellectual. She thought he was better looking on the computer screen than he was in person.

Elizabeth thanked him for the introduction. She began her presentation by saying, "One of the things I hate about this country is . . ." Then she read from a prepared statement without looking up. As she spoke it became clear that what she hated about this country was that not everyone saw things the way she did. Her hand made choppy gestures while she demonized the opposition, the loggers who opposed protecting the spotted owl on the grounds that protection cost them their jobs. Forest Watch was often accused of being a group of idle rich people indifferent to the needs of others to earn a living. In some respects Elizabeth's performance was that of a woman unwilling to make any concessions to the opposition or even to her audience. She seemed to have little experience with public speaking. Claire was an academic and academics learned how to speak before an audience, to look up and make eye contact, to pause for emphasis, to speak slowly and distinctly, to pace themselves. Speaking in public was how most academics earned their living. Environmentalists were more likely to be amateurs. Although people put money into the environmental movement, few took any out. Claire supposed Brian was paid a salary, but she doubted it was much of one.

In spite of the unprofessional presentation, the audience gravitated to Elizabeth after it was over. Her looks and her passion for her subject made her a magnet. Claire stood at the back of the room and waited while Elizabeth basked in the glow. She was conscious of time and didn't like to be left cooling her heels. As time passed she got annoyed. If it hadn't been so important for her to talk to Elizabeth, she might have walked out.

After Elizabeth had given everyone else their due, she looked up. "Claire," she said. "We were supposed to be having a drink, weren't we? I'm so sorry I forgot."

The remark had the effect of making Claire feel belittled, which she supposed was the intent. She wondered whether Elizabeth's rudeness was simple arrogance or the sign of an insecure person unconsciously seeking the rejection she felt she deserved. When it came to human motivation, Claire was more inclined to accept the complicated than the simple. If she had been trying to renew an acquaintance with Elizabeth, she would have gone no further, but motive and character were critical in the death of Evelyn Martin, so she swallowed her anger and asked, "Do you have time?"

Elizabeth looked at her watch. "I can give you half an hour."

"Let's go down to the bar," Claire said.

Elizabeth wasted precious minutes stopping to talk to people she saw on the way downstairs, but when they got to the bar, she spent an hour at a table with Claire. Elizabeth had an elastic sense of time that expanded when it served her own interests. They began by talking about the spotted owl. Claire was in agreement that endangered species should be protected whatever the cost. She thought Forest Watch's tactics were unnecessarily confrontational, but she didn't say so. Eventually she was able to direct Elizabeth's attention to Amaral's investigation.

"I assume asking about our alibis means he suspects one of us," Elizabeth said.

"That would be my assumption," Claire replied. "Did he give you a description of the woman the runner saw arguing with Evelyn?"

"No, but she must resemble us or why would he be asking for our alibis? The person he ought to be investigating is Miranda Kohl. She has a better motive than any of us do." She sampled the bar nuts, grimaced and said, "Too salty. Have you got anything else?" she asked the waiter, who went off to do her bidding.

"Amaral contacted Miranda," Claire said. "Her alibi is that she was on location in Mexico."

"How did he find out about her?"

"I told him," Claire admitted.

"You? Why?"

Claire felt that telling Elizabeth the truth would make her vulnerable, but lying was not her forte. She didn't trust herself to do it well. "Self-interest, I suppose. I don't have an alibi. I was home with my cat on April twenty-first."

"Really?" said Elizabeth, turning the spotlight of her attention on Claire. "Well then I can see why *you'd* want to direct Amaral's attention toward Miranda. I have a very good alibi myself." Her tone suggested she thought Claire was dim for not concocting her own alibi.

"To tell you the truth, it struck me as

rather convenient for you and for Ginny," Claire replied.

"Oh? Well, I was in Santa Fe at a Forest Watch seminar that day. I have a credit card receipt for dinner at the Santa Café."

"Which wouldn't prove you had dinner with Ginny."

"Ginny told you we had dinner together, didn't she?"

"Yes, and she was drinking when she said it."

The waiter came back with a bowl of unsalted nuts. Elizabeth sampled them and thanked him.

"Surely you've noticed that Ginny likes to drink."

"Was she drunk when you got together?"

Elizabeth shrugged. "Most likely."

"What time did you have dinner?"

"We started with drinks at five. Dinner went on till nine or ten o'clock, I'd say."

"That's a long time for you and Ginny to spend together."

"We had a lot of catching up to do."

"You sent her out into the dark after dinner and let her drive home drunk?"

"I suppose I did. She wouldn't have given me the car keys so what was I supposed to do? I wasn't prepared to wrestle them from her."

Claire believed that part of it — she couldn't imagine Elizabeth trying to wrestle the keys away from Ginny — but she didn't believe the two of them had enjoyed a long dinner.

"You ought to spend more time establishing your own innocence instead of questioning mine," Elizabeth said. "You're the one with no alibi."

Claire had noticed that Brian Duval was leaning against the doorway watching them and apparently waiting for the conversation to end. Elizabeth's back was to the door and she hadn't seen him yet.

"Brian Duval is here," Claire said.

"Is he?" Elizabeth smiled. "Are we done?" she asked.

"I'm done," Claire said.

"Me, too," Elizabeth replied. She stood up, went to the door and walked down the hall with Brian, leading Claire to think that was who she was having dinner with.

Claire had made plans to meet her coworker Celia Alegria at the KiMo Theatre, a short walk from the Hyatt, to see a production of *The Barber of Seville*. The drink with Elizabeth had taken longer than she expected and it was almost time for the show. She left her car downstairs in the Hyatt parking lot and walked to the KiMo, a wonderfully ornate theater and one of her favorite buildings in Albuquerque. The Duke City had miles of undistinguished architecture interspersed every now and then with a jewel-encrusted treasure like the KiMo.

Celia was waiting for Claire in the lobby. She always dressed with style, even at work. Tonight she was wearing a red velvet Navajo dress with a broomstick pleated skirt and a necklace made out of oversized silver beads. The color complimented her long black hair. Claire thought of Celia as a macaw among the sparrows at the library. She held her own in the KiMo.

"You look great," Claire said.

"You're looking good yourself," Celia replied.

"Me?" Claire wore a gray dress with an antique silver pin from Mexico. "I think I fit in better in the Hyatt than I do here. Here I feel like a plain Jane."

"Never think that," said Celia. She stepped back and examined Claire. "You have a simple style that works for you."

They entered the theater, took their seats and waited for the curtain to go up.

"How was your meeting with your friend?" Celia asked.

"All right. Elizabeth is a person who gets

her own way regardless of the effect on anyone else, one of those complicated people you either spend your lifetime trying to figure out or you run away from as fast as you can. She doesn't get along very well with women, but there's usually a man around willing to put up with her."

"Capable of murder?" Claire had confided in Celia her fears about the death of Evelyn Martin. She trusted Celia not to talk about it at work.

"Who? Elizabeth? Or the man?"

"Either one."

"I don't think the murder was a premeditated act. If it was committed in fear or anger or self-defense, I suppose Elizabeth was as capable as any of us. More capable, maybe, than some of us. She has a temper. As for a man, a woman was spotted at Evelyn's house the night she supposedly died." Considering that a man might have been involved cracked open a few doors in the house of Evelyn Martin's death, but the opera began and distracted Claire from opening them any wider.

Celia loved opera and her enthusiasm drew Claire in and left her feeling she'd been diverted and charmed for a few hours.

They walked to Celia's car, which she had parked near the theater. Celia gave Claire a ride back to the Hyatt, letting her off at the front door on Tijeras. Claire said good night and walked through the revolving door feeling she was leaving Albuquerque behind and entering another city, Phoenix, perhaps, which had its share of elegant hotels. She intended to walk across the lobby and take the elevator at the rear of the building to the underground parking lot. As she stepped from the revolving door, she saw Elizabeth and Brian walking toward the elevators that went up to the guest rooms. They were about the same height and they looked good together. Elizabeth whispered something in his ear and he laughed. The elevator door opened, then closed behind them.

Claire went to the elevator bank and watched the buttons to see where the elevator stopped. She took the next elevator to that floor feeling like a private eye tracking a philandering spouse. A convex mirror was mounted high in the elevator. She could see her reflection in the mirror, but the convexity distorted it enough to make her wonder if she was who she pretended to be, the quiet, intellectual Claire Reynier or a snoop who was following an old friend to a hotel assignation? She reminded herself that she was doing it because she was a murder suspect, not because she was a voyeur. Still she was embarrassed by the tingle of excitement she felt when the elevator reached the floor and the door opened. It was in her power to let the door close again and push the down button, but she didn't do it. She held the door open with her hand and, as discreetly as possible, peered into the hallway trying to think of some reasonable excuse if she was noticed.

She saw Elizabeth and Brian enter a room with their arms around each other, whispering and laughing. The door closed softly and clicked shut behind them. Claire took the elevator back down, all too aware of its sinking motion. She had witnessed something she had never experienced herself — the excitement of an illicit encounter in a hotel room. Sex in your own bed with your own mate was bound to seem dull in comparison. She felt flushed as she walked across the Hyatt lobby hoping no one would notice her. No one did. She took the elevator at the rear of the building down to the depths of the hotel parking lot. She didn't like underground lots, especially at night. Usually her antennae were out for shadows and suspicious people, but tonight her mind was full of what she had just witnessed. She got in her truck and drove home still under the erotic spell of Elizabeth and Brian.

★ ★ ★

It was too warm for a fire, almost warm enough to sleep with the window open. After Claire got into bed, she thought about opening it, but she didn't feel like getting out of bed again. As she drifted into the suburb surrounding the city of sleep, she had the sensation that Brian (or was that Jess?) was in bed with her. She didn't want either of those men. She didn't want John in her bed, and she certainly didn't want Evan back. Still it would be nice to have someone. For a while she had enjoyed the freedom and the room of sleeping alone, but by now her bed felt empty. It was an idle exercise, but she had no one to answer to so she indulged herself. If she could pick anyone in the world to bring to her bed, who would it be? She had been thinking so much about the years in the sorority house that her mind naturally gravitated to that time. She remembered the semester she had spent in Europe and North Africa at the beginning of her junior year. She remembered Pietro Antonelli, the Italian student she met in Spain. She left her girlfriends behind and traveled with him through Spain, Morocco, France and Italy. In many ways that had been the happiest period of her life. She loved Pietro's company, his spirit of adventure and his sense of humor. She liked the freedom of the open road and a day with no plans. But they quarreled in Venice and parted company. She returned to the U of A and met Evan. What had become of Pietro? she wondered as she drifted into a sleep surrounded not by a suburb but by a medina in Morocco with streets as narrow as alleys and souks where craftsmen were dying yarn and tanning leather.

In the morning she practiced tai chi, made a cup of coffee and took it into her courtyard. She needed to think and the walls of her courtyard were better for thinking than the riot of her rose garden. The green shoots of a datura plant were poking through the ground, and soon the courtyard would be putting on a performance of its own, but right now there was nothing to distract her from the sunlight, shadow and texture of her adobe wall. There wasn't any wind this morning. Claire stared at the line of demarcation where sunlight ended and shadow began and thought about what she had witnessed at the Hyatt. Elizabeth was having an affair with Brian. Maybe it was only a pleasant diversion when she came to New Mexico, food for her hungry ego, but she wouldn't want Jess to know about it. It was a rare person who wanted an affair to be discovered. She wondered if Brian was the good-looking man Ginny had seen Elizabeth with, not Jess. If Brian was the person Elizabeth had had dinner with, not Ginny. She was more likely to have spent several hours dining with Brian than with Ginny. She needed an alibi for that night. She might well have paid for the dinner with Brian, and she wouldn't want Jess to know she'd had dinner with him. She got to Ginny before Amaral did and concocted an alibi for both of them. It covered her, at least for the important part of the evening, but it didn't cover Ginny.

While Claire pondered the alibi issue, the shadow slid across her courtyard wall. Shadows caused by sunlight were always in motion. She blinked and focused on her own emotions. Was that sinking feeling she experienced when she saw Elizabeth and Brian enter the room the elevator shaft of envy? Was envy a natural response for women who had known each other thirty years ago? Would a woman always be comparing her condition in life to that of her former friends? Elizabeth had everything a woman might desire on the worldly plain. She had looks, money, children and sex, but she didn't have something that Claire valued — tranquility.

Chapter Twelve

When the other shoe dropped a few days later and Amaral showed up in her office, tranquility went out the window. Claire wasn't entirely surprised to see him. She knew the saying "be careful what you wish for because it might come true" could be revised to "be careful what you feared," because that also had a way of coming true. Once she saw Amaral, she realized that on a subliminal level she had been expecting him. She was working on the computer when she felt a shadow cross her window. Thinking it was Harrison, she didn't look up.

"Ms. Reynier?" Amaral said in his soft voice.

Claire spun around in her desk chair and saw him standing in the doorway. "Detective Amaral?" she asked. She considered it an invasion for him to come to her office without stopping at the information desk to announce his presence. "What are you doing here?"

He stepped into her office and stood in front of her desk while she remained seated. It gave him the advantage of towering over her, but she was too stunned to get up. "I have received information that *The Confidence-Man* you claimed was stolen from your house is here in your office."

"That's ridiculous," Claire said.

"May I take a look?"

"If you must."

The absurdity of this search allowed Claire to lean back in her chair while Amaral went to the bookshelves on the side wall to examine her books. When he didn't find what he was looking for, he turned toward the shelves on the wall behind Claire. His eyes looked across her shoulder and landed on one particular book.

"Would you hand me that copy of *The Scarlet Letter*, please?" he asked.

"I don't have a copy of *The Scarlet Letter*."

"Yes, you do." He reached over her shoulder, took a book from the shelf and showed Claire that it wore the jacket of the Modern Library edition of *The Scarlet Letter*.

"That's not my book," Claire protested.

Amaral ignored her while he removed the dust jacket, placed it on her desk, then displayed the spine of the book. It was bound in full brown morocco, gilt-stamped with raised bands. The golden letters read "*The Confidence-Man: His Masquerade* by Herman Melville."

"Good God," Claire said.

"There's no need to put on a performance for me, Ms. Reynier."

"I am *not* performing." Her shock at having *The Confidence-Man* appear in her office masquerading as *The Scarlet Letter* was genuine.

"My informant warned me that you were concealing your book beneath the cover of *The Scarlet Letter*."

"And who exactly is this informant?"

"I can't say."

"Do you suppose that the reason you found the book exactly where your informant said it would be is because your informant put it there? It was easy enough for you to walk in here unnoticed, wasn't it? Someone else did the same thing and put that book on my shelf when I was out." The task would have been even easier, Claire thought, if that person knew when she would be out.

"Don't you lock your door when you're not here?"

"Not necessarily," Claire said. People at the center were lax about security. The solidity of the massive Pueblo revival-style building made the people who worked there feel sheltered and safe. She had been robbed while at work, but the theft had been from her truck, not her office. "If that book is a first edition, it has been rebound. It wasn't originally printed with a full morocco binding and gilt letters," she said, trying to keep any hint of sarcasm from her voice. She didn't want to suggest that Amaral was ignorant about rare books, even though it happened to be true. "My book was in the original binding."

Amaral's eyes behind the wire-rimmed lenses were doubtful, and she realized that the only description he had of her book was the one she had given him. Unlike valuable paintings, books rarely came with a chain of title. She hadn't mentioned the binding when she described the book to him; she didn't think it was significant. She had mentioned Melville's signature, however.

"Would you open the book?" she asked him.

Amaral obliged.

"Go to the title page, please. That's the page where you should find Melville's signature, if this book has a signature."

Amaral turned to the page and showed it to Claire. She saw a signature that read "Herman Melville," but she wasn't convinced Melville had put it there. She needed to see it at closer range.

"May I examine it?" she asked Amaral. If

it was her book, it would already have her fingerprints on it, but if it wasn't she would be a fool to put them there. "I won't put any prints on it," she added. "I have gloves in my desk that we use when we examine rare and valuable documents."

Amaral agreed. She reached into her desk, took out a pair of white gloves, inserted her fingers into them and accepted the book, balancing it in her hands for a moment, sniffing it and feeling its weight. She closed her eyes; in Claire's experience, dulling one sense made the others more acute. Librarians often developed a sixth sense about books. Some believed they could tell where a book had been by its smell. Others could remember exactly where on a page they read something. Claire wasn't an expert on odors, but she thought this book had a vaguely musty smell, as if it had spent time in a damper place. Her books did not have a musty smell, but her *Confidence-Man* had been gone long enough to have picked up that odor somewhere else. It didn't take long, Claire knew, for a book to smell musty. She opened her eyes and studied the signature. Her first impression was that it was not Melville's signature and, therefore, not her book. But that was also what she wanted to believe, and she had to find a way to support her conclusion with logic.

"That's not an authentic signature," she said. "In fact it is a poor imitation."

"And why is that?" Amaral replied with amusement dancing behind his wire-rimmed lenses.

Before she answered him, she checked the copyright page and ascertained that this was the same edition as her book, although it couldn't be the same signature. "This book and mine were both published in 1857. This book has been rebound since then. Most likely my book was signed near the time it was published, but, if not, it was definitely signed in Melville's lifetime. He died in 1891. This isn't an old signature. The ink isn't faded or cracked as it would be in a book that was signed so long ago. The age of the ink would be enough to ascertain that Melville didn't sign it, but if you want further proof, this signature doesn't have the peaks and valleys of Melville's writing. It is not his *M*. It's not his *e*." Claire was winging this to some extent, working from memory since she didn't have an authentic signature in front of her for comparison. "Melville was a deep and complicated man. This is the signature of a more shallow person. I know a handwriting expert in Santa Fe quite capable of proving this signature is a fraud. I'd be happy to give you his name if you're not willing to accept my opinion."

"Would an expert you recommend be capable of giving an unbiased opinion, Ms. Reynier?" Amaral's precise way of speaking had become intimidating. Instead of smoothing and polishing his words before he released them, he seemed to be dicing them with a knife, a knife that was wrapped in a velvety smooth scabbard, but still a knife.

"Yes. Reputation is everything in his business. But if you don't trust him, find somebody else. There are a number of experts capable of establishing that signature is a fraud." The temperature was rising in her voice. She tried to lower the volume so as not to let Amaral know how angry she was or attract the attention of anyone passing by.

"And if someone were to establish that signature is a fraud, what would that prove?" he asked.

"That this book is not my *Confidence-Man*."

"Isn't it possible the signature in your book was a fraud?"

"I wouldn't have a book in my house that was a fraud."

"Do you have any documentation to prove that?"

All Claire had for authentication was the word of the person who sold it to her twenty years ago, a book dealer she knew then and trusted, a book dealer who was now dead. "Not really."

"Are you aware that your book was the only object on Evelyn Martin's list that was not found in her house?"

"If you're implying that I went to her house and took my book back, you're wrong. This is not my book. I never went to see Evelyn Martin. I was never in her house. Even if I took the book, which I didn't, I wouldn't be dumb enough to keep it in my office."

"It was well hidden, though, wasn't it?"

Amaral seemed to be enjoying this investigation, reminding Claire of a comment she once heard from a former Albuquerque policewoman that she was thrilled when she found a criminal who had given a crime more than five minutes' thought. Whoever had perpetrated this hoax had given it considerable thought. The author of *The Scarlet Letter* was Nathaniel Hawthorne, Herman Melville's neighbor near Pittsfield, Massachusetts. It was a fact that might be known to anyone who had taken a college-level course in American lit, but apparently not to the detective. Claire didn't think it would serve her purpose to tell him.

"That book was hidden from me, perhaps, but not from you," she said. "You knew exactly where to look; but I had no idea it was on my shelf. Someone is trying to frame me. If you could find that person, you would find your murderer. Test the book for fingerprints. If it was the book that Evelyn stole, you should find her fingerprints on it. You won't find mine on it, because I never owned that book."

"We would like to have your fingerprints on file for comparison, but lack of fingerprints on the book won't prove that it is not your copy."

"Why not?" asked Claire.

"You were wearing white gloves when you handled it here. You were wearing white gloves when you handled it at home."

Claire looked down at her hands still encased in the type of gloves debutantes wore to coming-out parties, gloves that made her appear young and foolish, gloves that she had put on voluntarily. She felt as if she had just put her fingers into quicksand. Every move she made to escape had the effect of sinking her deeper. The time she had been dreading had arrived. The time had come to hire a lawyer.

"I won't talk to you any further until I have a lawyer," she said.

"That's your prerogative. Please ask whoever you hire to get in touch with me." He paused and looked over the top of his wire-rimmed glasses. "I'm sure whoever that is will advise you to have no further contact with the witness, Ms. Reynier."

Claire considered that remark the parting slice of the knife.

Amaral picked up the book, put the *Scarlet Letter* jacket back on, inserted it in a clear-plastic evidence bag and walked out of her office, nearly colliding with Harrison Hough in the hallway.

"Excuse me," Harrison said. "Have we met? I am Harrison Hough, the director of the center."

"Detective Dante Amaral with the Santa Fe Police Department," he said, extending his hand.

"My pleasure," Harrison replied. He shook Amaral's hand then continued down the hallway, acting as if he had very important matters on his mind. Claire knew she would hear from him later.

She shut the door, closed the blinds and sat down at her desk. The books on her walls that fueled her imagination and pro-vided insulation from the outer world no longer seemed so inspiring or comforting. In fact she had the sensation that they were closing in on her. She felt that if she stayed in her office one minute longer the books would tumble from the shelves and bury her under the pages. She got up and left the office, locking her door behind her. She walked down the hallway and through the wrought-iron door of the center without seeing anyone. All the offices she passed were empty. Usually she walked out past the information desk that faced the Anderson Reading Room and through the gallery. Today she took the other route, down the hallway past the Willard Reading Room and the murals that were considered racist. At the end of the hallway she turned right, walked down another hallway that led past restrooms and a shop where the library sold books they no longer wanted. This path led her to an exterior door. It was a path anyone could have taken to reach her office unno-ticed. It would have required only seconds to place the bogus *Scarlet Letter* on her shelf. If the person had been noticed or caught, she could have said she was a friend leaving a gift for Claire. Although "acquaintance" would be a more accurate word. A friend would not be framing her for murder. Claire had no doubt that it was either someone she knew — someone who had also been a suspect in the death of Evelyn Martin — or that person's representative.

She thought about Ginny, Elizabeth, Miranda and Lynn. All had motives. All had means. Elizabeth had been in Albuquerque. Ginny lived nearby. Lynn and Miranda were quite capable of getting to Albuquerque if need be. They had all provided Amaral with alibis for the night in question. All of them could know by now that she didn't have an alibi. Either she had told them herself or they had told each other. They all knew Evelyn had stolen her copy of *The Confidence-Man*. She hadn't told Miranda to her face but she had told her husband, Erwin. It might be expensive for someone to locate a first edition, but it wasn't impossible.

She went out the door, circled around the building to the duck pond and sat down on the ground. The massive walls of the library kept it connected to the earth, but it had a tower that reached for the sky. It was the university's signature building. Claire looked into the water and watched the tower's reflection ripple and shift. All she had to do to set it in motion was disturb the surface tension by tossing something into the water. She picked up a stone, threw it in the pond and watched the tower dissolve under the impact. She believed that a signature could reflect the state of mind of the author. If that were the case, what would her state of mind — which was currently as muddled as the tower's reflection — do to the memory of a signature? Now that she was out of her office, she wasn't as confident about the signature as she had been in front of Amaral. She had accepted the original as Melville's because she trusted the dealer she bought it from, but she had never examined the signature. How could she be so positive the book Amaral had wasn't her book rebound in full brown morocco? And if it wasn't, where was her book? Evelyn must have disposed of it in some way. If she had sold it, it should turn up sooner or later, unless it ended up in the hands of a collector who just stuck it on a shelf. She waited until the water settled down and the reflection of the tower mirrored the original, then she went back to her office and called the three dealers she knew.

When she asked if they had heard anything about the book, the answers were no, no, and no, but they all told her that Amaral had been in touch with them and they would have to notify him if the book surfaced. No one had sold an unsigned first edition recently. No one had seen one rebound in full brown morocco. Only Brett Moon had anything new to pass on.

"Your boss called and told me that if I ever came across a signed first edition of *The Confidence-Man*, he'd like to buy it no matter what the price."

"Harrison said that?" Claire knew she worked in a backstabbing profession, but she hadn't anticipated this particular stab. "You know that if you do come across one, it will be my book."

"I told him that. He said he would discuss it with you at the time."

"Thanks for letting me know," Claire said.

"Glad to help," Brett replied.

Claire pondered this latest betrayal. Harrison had already told her of his interest in the book. He had no right to go around her back to Brett Moon. To be fair, all Harrison knew was that a valuable book had been stolen from her. He didn't know Claire was the subject of a murder investigation unless someone else had told him. Claire knew she would have to confront Harrison sooner or later. She locked her door and walked down the hall to his office.

She found him at his desk writing on a legal pad. Claire had seen enough of his handwriting to know that it was small, cramped and pinched, reflecting his permanently sour mood. On the shelf behind his desk he had a folk art sculpture of death pulling a cart. To Claire it appeared to be floating over his head like the clouds floating over the heads of characters in comic books. She saw it as a hieroglyphic expressing Harrison's gloomy state of mind.

Before he could say a word, she said, "Brett Moon told me you asked him to let you know if he found a signed first edition of *The Confidence-Man*. If that book shows up, Harrison, it will be *my* book."

"Did you own the only signed first edition in existence?" he asked.

"Not the only one, but there are very few and mine has probably been sold recently."

Harrison picked up a letter opener that lay on his desk and began turning it over in his fingers. "What was that book that Detective Amaral was holding?"

"It was a signed first edition of *The Confidence-Man*, but it wasn't my book."

"How do you know?"

"The binding was different. The signature was fraudulent."

"Where did Amaral get it?"

"Someone hid it in my office, then told him it was there."

"It had a dust jacket, didn't it?"

"Yes. The person who put it in my office hid it behind a *Scarlet Letter* dust jacket."

"Interesting place to conceal it. Did you know that Hawthorne was Melville's neighbor?"

"Of course," Claire said.

"Let me make sure I understand." Harrison poked the desk with the tip of his pen. "Someone took an authentic signed first edition from your house and someone else put a book with a forged signature in your office?"

"Yes," Claire replied, realizing how absurd it sounded.

"I would say whoever did that had a lot of confidence but not much common sense."

It was his attempt at a joke, but Claire didn't laugh. She knew she would have to tell him the whole story now. He had met Amaral; he could contact the detective directly if he chose to. "Evelyn Martin, the woman who stole the book from me, was found murdered in her house in Santa Fe. She also stole from some other friends. One of them is trying to frame me by making it appear that I went to her house and took my book back."

Harrison's mind made the leap she had expected it would. He wasn't dumb, just dull. His mind tended to get stuck in well-worn ruts. "*You* are the subject of a murder investigation?" he asked. His tone was incredulous, but he didn't seem to be blaming her. To the contrary, he seemed intrigued. His eyes had that light that comes from curiosity about another human being, a light that Claire rarely saw in Harrison's eyes.

"I am," Claire admitted. "But I intend to hire a lawyer. I'm sure it will all be cleared up."

"I never would have suspected you would be capable of murder."

"Thanks for the vote of confidence."

"Are you aware that the subject of *The Confidence-Man* is the existential enigma of the self?"

"Yes," Claire replied, "so you said."

"And now you have become an enigma yourself."

"Not to me. I know who I am." In her mind Claire finished that phrase with *and I know what I have accomplished.* "On the other hand, Evelyn Martin and the other women she robbed have become enigmas to me," she said. It was a more personal and revealing comment than she had ever made to Harrison.

"And one of them is framing you?"

"Most likely," Claire said.

"That's rather insidiously implicative."

It was another one of those vaguely familiar phrases that Harrison used, but to Claire's surprise he seemed to be supporting her. She'd been afraid that his discovering she'd been accused of murder might cost her her job.

"Keep me informed," Harrison said. "If the detective needs a character reference, I will be happy to provide one."

"Thank you," Claire said. She walked back to her office feeling buoyed by Harrison's support.

Claire's dreams were often puzzles with words for clues. Sometimes she solved the puzzles in her dreams; more often she did not. That night she had a dream in which she saw the words *existential enigma* in a handwriting that was cramped and pinched. She woke up with the puzzle unsolved but the words on her mind and a recollection of where she might have seen them. She went to her office, turned on the reading light and looked through the Oxford edition of *The Confidence-Man* with the introduction by Jeffrey Omer. She skimmed it like a stone skipping across water, hopping from paragraph to paragraph until the phrase "existential enigma of the self" leapt out at her. She continued skimming until she found the phrase "insidiously implicative," as well as numerous "to be sure's." Jeffrey Omer was a middle-aged critic when Harrison was a young graduate student. Had Harrison read Omer's work so often that certain phrases got stuck in his mind? If that was the case, he'd gotten far more intimate with his source than a scholar ought to be. Harrison was turning out to be another enigma wrapped in a riddle. With her mind full of questions, Claire went back to bed and wrapped herself in sleep.

Chapter Thirteen

When she got to work in the morning, Claire called Sally Froelich, a lawyer who had represented her on another matter.

"How are you?" Sally asked.

"All right," Claire replied.

"Are things going well at the center?"

"Yes and no," Claire replied. "Work is fine, but I'm the subject of a murder investigation."

"You?"

"Me."

"How on earth did that happen?"

Claire explained.

"I would love to represent you," Sally said, "but I don't do criminal law. My specialty is wills and probate, stiffs and gifts. I can recommend someone if you like."

"Please," Claire said.

Sally gave her the name of Sid Hyland, a well-known criminal lawyer seen often on TV.

"Do you think he would represent me?" she asked. "I'm not exactly a high-profile client."

"Not all of Sid's clients make the evening news. I think he'll be intrigued by you.

You're a better class of suspect than he usually gets. Sid's a cowboy and he can be overbearing, but he's one of the best criminal lawyers in town. If I were you, I'd give him a chance."

Sid Hyland lived up to his reputation as a cowboy by wearing jeans, cowboy boots and a bolo tie on the day Claire met him in his office. She was sure that when he left the office, he'd put on the cowboy hat lying on top of his bookcase. She noticed that the bookcase contained nothing but legal books. If he was a reader, his office gave no evidence of that fact. Sid's office was rather spare, unlike Sally's, which was as comfortable as a living room. He had a diploma from UNM Law School on the wall, a massive wooden desk stained dark brown, the bookshelves — also stained dark brown — and that was it. His gray hair skimmed the edge of his collar. He was a big man, long legged and broad shouldered. Claire thought that one day she would meet a big man secure enough that he felt no need to dominate, a man as large and gentle as a bear, but it wasn't Sid Hyland. Like other big men Claire had known, he dominated the room and the conversation. Listening ought to be a useful skill for a defense attorney, but it was a skill Hyland appeared not to have developed. He seemed more interested in the sound of his own voice than he did in hers. Halfway through her comments his attention wandered, and once that happened Claire's sentences began to droop and lose their focus. She supposed his forceful manner would be effective at intimidating the prosecution and the jury, but hoped it wasn't the only note he knew how to play. Intimidation might not be the best strategy with Amaral. Beneath his deferential manner, the detective was a man capable of sidling away from other people's agendas.

"Now tell me why a classy lady like yourself would be accused of murder," Hyland said.

As Claire attempted to tell him, he peppered the conversation with interruptions and advice. She should have hired him sooner. She should never have talked to Amaral without a lawyer. She shouldn't have let Amaral into her office. She should have insisted he get a warrant before she let him take the book.

Claire supposed Hyland would bill her by the minute or a fraction thereof. She struggled to get her story out and to make herself understood.

"I met Amaral's witness, and —"

"You met the witness?" he asked, leaning forward and making her want to back her chair away, the same way a prosecutor could make her feel. "How did that happen?"

"I went to the house at the time of day I was supposed to have —"

"What time was that?"

"Dusk. A woman ran by. I stopped her and asked —"

"What did she see?"

"A woman with frosted hair who could have been any of us. But she said one woman was a size fourteen and the other a twelve."

"What size are you?"

"Ten."

"It's not wise to talk to a witness. The prosecution could accuse you of putting words in her mouth."

"It won't happen again. I don't think she'll make a good witness for the prosecution."

"Why not?"

"It was dusk, there were a lot of shadows, she couldn't see that well. A defense attorney should be able to make something out of that on the witness stand."

"My object is not to put anyone on the

witness stand. You may have seen me on the evening news, but most of the people I represent never go to trial. Here you have a badly decomposed body discovered weeks later, making it impossible for the prosecution to establish an exact time of death. Nevertheless it would be helpful if you had an alibi for the evening the runner saw the women arguing."

"I was home alone."

"Did you make any long-distance phone calls? Speak to someone who could confirm your whereabouts?"

"I'll check my bill. I don't believe some of the other suspects' alibis. Elizabeth and Ginny claim they had dinner together in Santa Fe. Elizabeth has a credit card receipt, but I doubt she had dinner with Ginny. They don't like each other. I think Elizabeth actually had dinner with a lover in Santa Fe but doesn't want her lover in Tucson to know. That leaves Ginny with no alibi. Miranda Kohl claims she was on location, but I don't know how Amaral established that fact. Miranda is an actress filming a new TV series and —"

"What about the other woman?"

"Lynn? She says she was home with her husband."

"In my experience a significant other will

do anything possible to protect a mate. It's quite a complicated scheme to find another copy of *The Confidence-Man*, fake a signature, then hide that book in your office. It's possible that whoever is trying to frame you had help and the help came from a husband or a lover."

Until now that thought had been as ephemeral as a moth outside the window, a possibility Claire had not wanted to consider. Hearing Hyland put it into words made her realize it was a possibility she had to consider.

"If that isn't your book, what do you suppose happened to your copy of *The Confidence-Man*?"

"I assume that Evelyn sold it, and I'm hoping that sooner or later it will turn up on the rare book market."

"It would help if we could find it. Presumably Evelyn's prints and your prints will be on it to establish chain of custody and ownership. Are your prints on the book that was found in your office?"

"I wore gloves when I handled it."

Hyland leaned back in his chair and crossed the foot of one leg over the thigh of the other. He turned his full attention on Claire and she saw how powerful a force it could be when focused. "Is there any possibility your fingerprints will be found in the victim's house?" he asked.

"It's possible I touched a wall or a window outside, but I never went inside," Claire said. "Evelyn could have taken something else from my house. A glass, for example, or a pencil, something I wouldn't have missed that had my fingerprints on it."

"I won't allow Amaral to fingerprint you until he charges you, and my goal is to prevent him from charging you. At the moment I think his case is weak."

"Is there anything I can do to clear my name? Waiting for Amaral to come after me is a very uncomfortable feeling."

"I suggest you concentrate on your job and leave my job to me."

He stood up and shook Claire's hand, making it clear that the meeting was over.

When she got home that night she went outside and watched Venus slipping into view above the West Mesa. It was the dark of the moon, the best time to see Venus. Even the lights of the city didn't dim its power. She pondered her conversation with Sid Hyland. Considering the men in her friends' lives as accomplices added a layer of complexity to the investigation and left her wondering whether any of *them* were capable of murder or fraud.

The only suspects who had no man to aid or abet them were Claire herself and Ginny, who remained a puzzle. Was she a drunk or just pretending to be? In a sense inebriation was always a performance. They had gone to school in a time when young women masked their intelligence, but Claire had never thought Ginny was stupid. She had the intelligence to plan the book-in-the-office scheme, but was she devious enough to carry it out? It was a question Claire couldn't answer without knowing whether Ginny was a real drunk or a fake.

She remembered what Sid Hyland said about turning her defense over to him. She should be relieved to place her burdens on his broad shoulders, but doing nothing meant she had to live with the ominous threat that sooner or later Amaral would come up with something even more incriminating, something she had overlooked or someone else had inserted. It would be difficult to prove in court that the murder took place on the night in question, but most likely it had happened then.

Claire went inside to her office, found her phone bill for the month of April and discovered that she had made no long-distance calls that night. There was nothing to prove she had been at home. Since she was already sitting at her desk in front of her computer, she decided to take a look at CultureVulture.com, the Web site Ginny wrote for. She typed in the URL. The Web site came up and a vulture appeared on her screen, cawed and flapped its wings. As Ginny had said, the site covered cultural events. Claire negotiated her way to the listings for Santa Fe, searched the Gerald Peters Gallery and found a description for the Renata Jennings show that was credited to Ginny Bogardus.

"What can you say about abstractions?" it read.

They're red, they're black, they're a circle, they're a square, they're the very absence of pictureness. Forget about Renata Jennings's black phase. The black paintings in this show are stuck in the box. By now haven't we learned all there is to learn from black? Black is punctuation — the comma, the period, the semicolon, the pause in the flow. Red is the now. Red *is* the flow. Red is the fiery breath of the dragon. The paintings in Jennings's red series swirl and whirl and dissolve the boundary of the box. They suck the strength from the viewer and leave you gasping on some subtly reptilian level of consciousness. Skip the black. Red is the reason for this show, the only reason for this show.

It had a certain bravura style that Claire found amusing, but it was an exaggeration of the show she had seen, reminding her that the written word had always been the perfect forum for a literary con artist.

Before she went to bed she went outside and lured Nemesis in with a dish of tuna. Venus, no longer alone in the sky, had been surrounded and diminished by a multitude of pinholes in the darkness.

When Claire got to work in the morning, she took a step down one of the paths that began when Evelyn Martin left Jeffrey Omer's critical analysis of Melville on her shelf. She supposed that leaving that book was Evelyn's idea of a joke. Presumably she had found it in a used bookstore somewhere; it had the beaten and battered look of a book that had been around. It was cheap, it was available, it was on the subject of the book she was stealing. The fact that it was that particular book could be considered serendipity or more bad luck. It was leading Claire to question the credibility of her boss, but then she was in a mood to question the credibility of everyone she knew.

She logged on to her computer, went to Dissertations Abstracts, located Harrison Hough's dissertation on Herman Melville and ordered a copy to be sent to her home address. It was something any scholar could do, but rarely would do without ulterior motive. If Harrison had gotten his Ph.D. from UNM, his dissertation would be in the library, but his doctorate was from UTEP. Fortunately Harrison was out that day so she didn't have to feel guilty every time she ran into him.

When she got home on Friday, she found a package lying on the brick floor of her courtyard. She went to her office, took the critical edition of *The Confidence-Man* from the shelf and brought it back outside. By now the days were long enough for her to sit on the banco in the evening and read. She opened the package and began the process of comparing the critical introduction to the dissertation. Normally, comparing a dissertation to anything went beyond boring, but this task had the thrill of the hunt, giving her the heightened alertness of a predator closing in on a prey, which might be exactly the way someone else was feeling about her. A transference took place between the hunter and the hunted, and she soon saw one between the doctoral candidate and the critic. The repetition in the phraseology was more than coincidental. In addition to "existential enigma of the self" and "insidiously implicative," she found "ontologically amorphous" and other phrases she had heard Harrison use. Harrison and Jeffrey Omer had reached similar conclusions, but well-meaning students of Melville might logically reach similar conclusions. Using the exact same language, however, would be considered plagiarism. While paraphrasing was acceptable, copying was not. Claire wondered whether Harrison had studied Omer so intently that the critic's phrases wore a channel in his brain and became his phrases. It was hard to imagine Harrison being dumb enough to steal deliberately from Jeffrey Omer, but it might happen unconsciously to someone who lacked an inventive mind. The committee at UTEP had been lax when they accepted the dissertation. Harrison's adviser should have been familiar with Omer's work.

While Claire had been reading, the shadows took over her courtyard. She put the dissertation and the book down on the banco and watched the shadows come to life on the summer wind. Nemesis climbed to the top of the wall and stood still, silhouetted against the fading light. Something rustled in the courtyard and he leapt for it, disappearing among the shadows. It was the hour when the coyotes came out of the Sandias into the foothills and began to hunt. There was the moment when a predator killed a prey and there was an instant right before the kill when the prey was there for the taking. Claire wondered which moment the predator found most gratifying. Harrison had stepped into her line of fire. She had enough evidence in these documents to ruin his career. Was she capable of doing it? What kind of a burden would it be to know it and not do it? Would she have to think "plagiarist" every time she looked at Harrison? The civilized action when in doubt was to discuss it. She picked up the documents, coaxed Nemesis inside and shut the door behind her.

Usually when she was troubled by something to do with books she ran it by John Harlan. She called him at home and was pleased to get the man and not the machine.

"Claire," he said, "how have you been?"

"I just discovered something I'd like to

talk to you about. I found evidence that Harrison plagiarized some of his dissertation on Melville."

"Well, that doesn't surprise me. That pompous pooh-bah never had an original thought," John replied. "Have you had dinner yet?"

Claire looked at her watch, which read eight o'clock. She thought about what was in her refrigerator — very little. "Not yet," she admitted.

"I'm fixing myself some gruel. Would you like to come over and share it? There's more than enough for two."

"It's getting late."

"What the hell, it's Friday night, isn't it? You don't have to work tomorrow."

Claire had forgotten that it was Friday. It had been one of those weeks when she was too preoccupied to remember the weekend was approaching. She had made no plans and faced the wasteland of no one to see and nowhere to go. The feeling hung over from high school that it was okay to stay home alone with your cat during the week, but to stay home on the weekend was pathetic. She accepted John's invitation.

She knew he lived in a townhouse complex near the store, but she had never actually been there. It was only an eight-minute drive from Claire's house, but much farther away in feeling. Albuquerque comprised fifteen hundred feet in elevation and several life zones beginning with the Rio Grande, which nourished a bosque of magnificent cottonwood trees. Claire lived at the high end of the city near where private land ended and national forest began. The natural vegetation here — prickly pear and cholla — was full of thorns, but a few hundred feet higher it turned to piñon and juniper. In her development people were changing the vegetation by planting lilacs and cottonwoods, and she herself had a wall of roses. The Heights and the Valley both had natural beauty and spectacular views, and that was where people with money tended to live. There was some fine architecture around the university and the downtown area, but in much of Albuquerque scrubby desert had been replaced by undistinguished buildings and unnatural vegetation.

The complex where John lived fell into the undistinguished category. It was a row of attached townhouses stuccoed in a forgettable color and had no landscaping or views. Claire knew why John had chosen to live here — he could afford it, it was convenient to work, he didn't have to think about it. John didn't care where he lived as long as he had his books. When he opened the door, Claire saw that his townhouse had the same careless clutter as his office. The walls were lined with bookcases. Papers were piled everywhere. The sofa was upholstered in gray, as was the armchair. His artwork consisted of black-and-white drawings, carelessly framed, haphazardly hung. The lighting came from overhead fixtures that made Claire feel as if she was being examined. Someone needed to tell John about plush furniture, pink bulbs, the welcoming puddle of light that seeped out from under a table lamp. Claire had to ask herself why she should expect plush furniture and pink bulbs from John when she didn't have them in her own house.

He had a warm glow when he met her at the door, and so did the amber liquid in the glass in his hand.

"What are you drinking?" Claire asked after they had exchanged their hellos.

"Jack Daniels. Would you like a shot?"

"A small one, on ice."

She followed him into the kitchen, separated from the living room by a counter and a dining room table. Like many other surfaces in the house, the table was piled high with reading material. John had cleared space enough for two and put down place mats with knives and forks. He dropped some ice in a glass and poured the Jack Daniels over it. Claire leaned against the counter and took a sip, enjoying the warm, mellow taste. The only time she had gotten drunk in recent memory was on Jack Daniels.

"Well, now that you know your boss is a plagiarist, what are you going to do about it?" John asked.

"I haven't decided."

"You never liked the guy, did you?"

"Not much. You know him. You know how difficult he can be. How parsimonious he is with money and praise."

"You could get him fired, couldn't you? It would make your life easier."

"It's not that easy to get someone fired. Harrison has tenure."

"They could move him sideways, let him keep his salary but give him an office in the basement with nothing to do. It would get him out of your hair."

"True."

"Dinner's almost ready, why don't we eat now, talk later?"

"All right," Claire said.

John concentrated on putting the chicken breasts in the microwave and the broccoli in the steamer. In a few minutes dinner was ready. He placed it on two plates with white rice he had already cooked and they carried it to the table. Like many men who found themselves single after having been married for a long time, John had a limited knowledge of cooking. The meal was edible but uninspired. Claire sipped at her Jack Daniels through dinner and imagined that she was eating chicken the way she prepared it, the way John didn't like it, roasted slowly in a clay pot with curry powder and onions and yams.

When the meal was over, John cleared the table and suggested they move to the living room, where they sat down at opposite ends of the sofa. John put his feet on the coffee table, stretched his arm across the back of the sofa and studied Claire, who kept wishing that he would turn the overhead lights off but feared he would misunderstand if she made the suggestion.

"Now tell me why you're so reluctant to nail your boss's ass to the wall," he said.

"Kindness?"

"Why don't I believe that's all there is to it? Not to say you're not a kind person, but you're not a simple person either."

"There are a number of things. I wouldn't want to be remembered as the vindictive librarian who destroyed Harrison Hough's career."

"Could you do it anonymously?"

"I could, but it seems like a cheap shot."

"Won't it be awkward to be working with the guy, seeing him every day, knowing what he did and not saying anything about it?"

"Yes," Claire replied. "Which is one reason I don't know what to do." She took a deep sip of her Jack Daniels, leaving a thimbleful of amber in the glass.

"Care for another?" John asked.

"No, thanks. I'm learning what it's like to be a rabbit with a hawk circling overhead myself, to have someone out to destroy my reputation and my life. Someone I know is trying to frame me for Evelyn Martin's murder."

"She's the woman who stole your *Confidence-Man*?"

"Right. Somebody hid another one in my office disguised under the jacket of *The Scarlet Letter*, then told the detective who is investigating me exactly where it was. It was a first edition and a signed copy, but it wasn't my book."

"How do you know?"

"The signature looked bogus."

"Couldn't the detective have it authenticated?"

"He could and he might, but he says that wouldn't prove anything. According to him my edition could have had a fraudulent signature. Apparently he believes I hit Evelyn Martin over the head, killed her, took my book back and hid it in my office."

"If you'd done that, you wouldn't be dumb enough to tell someone like me who could rat on you."

"Amaral doesn't have such a high opinion of my intelligence. I told him I wouldn't be dumb enough to own a book with a fraudulent signature either. On the night Evelyn Martin was presumed murdered, a runner saw a woman who fits my description arguing with her. I don't have an alibi for that night, so I've hired a lawyer. If this goes to court maybe I'll use you as a character witness."

John sipped at his drink. "Use me as your alibi. We're two people who are often home alone at night. Who's to say we weren't together?"

"Thanks, John. It's kind of you to offer, but neither one of us are practiced liars and we're liable to get ourselves into more trouble."

"I doubt it will ever go to court, but if it does, what jury in its right mind will believe you're capable of murder?"

"Isn't everyone capable of murder under the right circumstances?" Claire asked. "Suppose one of my former friends found out Evelyn had ripped her off and went to her house. There was an argument. Evelyn attacked the woman, who found a blunt object near her hand and hit Evelyn over the head with it. She didn't intend to kill anyone, just to protect herself."

"If someone did that she ought to come forward and say so."

John put his glass down on the end table and inched closer on the sofa, leading Claire to think that not only were most people capable of murder under the right circumstances, they were also capable of sex.

"Would you say so if you were guilty?" she asked him.

"I'd like to think I would. Self-defense isn't a crime."

"There would only be the perpetrator's word for it. Some of my former friends are not as civilized as you are. One of them is finding it easier to fake an alibi and implicate the person who doesn't have one — me."

He extended his arm along the back of the couch. Claire thought this might be the signal for her to move closer, too, and snuggle into his extended arm, but she remained committed to her end of the sofa. Dating had been awkward as a teenager. Dating in middle age was even worse. She had the same anxiety about how she would perform, but it wasn't fueled by the same wild animal desire. Desire at this age was more like a house pet that got to run wild only when permitted.

She glanced at her watch and said, "It's getting late," which was roughly the equivalent of declaring she had AIDS or wore a chastity belt.

She expected John to protest, but he surprised her by agreeing. He stood up. So did she. He walked her to the door, gave her a peck on the cheek and said good-bye.

"Thanks for the dinner," she said, pecking him back.

"My pleasure," he replied.

Later that night she woke up, well aware that she still had desire, although the man who'd been in her dreams was not John Harlan, as he appeared now, but Pietro Antonelli, as he was thirty years ago.

Chapter Fourteen

In the morning she took out a blank piece of paper, sat down at the table in her dining area, imagined herself to be a police artist and attempted to reconstruct Pietro's face as it might appear now. There was likely to be less hair on top of his head. When she knew him he had thick, reddish brown hair worn long. It was one of many things she admired about him. Pietro had been so skinny then that she felt his bones when they hugged. Reminding herself that Pietro would be in his fifties now, she added pounds to her mental image and began mentally manipulating the hair, moving the hairline back, changing the color from dark red to pale red to gray to white. Often as a man lost the hair from his head, he added it to his face. If the middle-aged Pietro had a beard, would it be short? Long? Gray? Red? White? His eyes at least were likely to remain the same: shrewd, warm, sparkling. After she rearranged the features, it was no longer the Pietro who inhabited her dreams. But she wouldn't be the Claire who inhabited his dreams either — if she even entered his dreams.

Feeling discouraged, she crumpled up

that piece of paper and threw it away. She got up, made herself a cup of coffee, sat down at the table again and tried to imagine the last face Evelyn Martin ever saw. Elizabeth Best's came out red and twisted in anger. Ginny's was also red, swollen and befuddled by alcohol. Claire didn't want to imagine Lynn's face here at all, but she made herself do it and came up with a sad, perplexed expression. As for Miranda, she saw her as the young woman, the old woman, the businesswoman, but no matter how hard she tried she couldn't get rid of the vague hippie expression she remembered from the U of A.

Considering what Sid Hyland had said, she moved on to the men in these women's lives. Brian and Jess were not so different from each other in their eagerness to please Elizabeth. She saw Steve Granger as thin, pale and hungry, and Erwin Bush as a card player with an amused glint in his eye.

Mentally she erased all of them, then took a blank piece of paper and drew the outline of another face, one with no hair, no eyes, no expression, merely a line around a blank, white space.

She set that piece of paper aside and thought about Harrison. Knowing all too well how he looked today, she tried to imagine how he looked in his late twenties or so, the age when he would have written his dissertation. Harrison remained Harrison, sour, mean-spirited, but suddenly vulnerable.

She thought about the phrase "the existential enigma of the self" and wrote it down. Technically the phrase wasn't Harrison's, but he had expropriated it.

Since words were the tools of her trade, Claire thought that she might learn more about the people she knew if she considered their words rather than their appearances. She began making a list of their more revealing phrases beginning with Evelyn's envious "look at *you,* aren't *you* doing well." She added Elizabeth's "one of the things I hate about this country," which expressed her out-of-touch self-centeredness. There was the naïve devotion expressed in Jess's "of course you were," the equally naïve admiration in Brian's "one of the foremost environmentalists in the Southwest." There were all the nicknames Ginny used in speech — Clairier, Lizzie, Evie — and the artbabble in her writing. Words were a smokescreen for Ginny, but she could wield them like a sword when she chose to. When she came to Lynn, Claire wrote down "I know you wouldn't do anything wrong," which expressed the concern she had for others. She remembered Steve saying Evelyn should move to Santa Fe, which expressed the acuteness of his observation. There hadn't actually been any dialogue with Miranda, only the written words in the e-mail. She remembered two phrases in that e-mail — "time wounds all heels" and "living well is the best revenge." She compared the latter phrase to Erwin's "revenge is a dish best served cold." Was this a case of two people who knew each other well falling into the same phraseology? Would the Miranda she knew have thought about revenge? But, of course, she had to consider that the Miranda who wrote this e-mail was no longer the person she had known, just as she was no longer the person Miranda had known.

Next she considered Amaral's precision with words, and Sid Hyland's "concentrate on your job and leave my job to me." Today was Saturday and she didn't have to consider her job. She had all day to do whatever she wanted to do, but before she made plans for the rest of the weekend, she added one more phrase to her list, Pietro's *cara mia, te amo.* " It was a beautiful phrase in sound and in spirit, far more lyrical than the occasional stilted "I love you" she had coaxed out of

Evan. She put all the papers in a manila folder and filed it in her desk. The file contained more questions than answers, but she was willing to put the questions aside and give the answers time to develop.

Turning her attention to what to do with the rest of the weekend, Claire checked her calendar and found two blank pages for Saturday and Sunday. She began poking through the pile of mail and newspapers on her desk to see if she could find something interesting to do. In the mail she found an invitation to the Rocky Mountain Booksellers annual dinner in Santa Fe that night. The booksellers who would be there were people she felt comfortable with. The hour drive to Santa Fe was a good chance to think.

The Rocky Mountain Booksellers dinner was held in a motel on Cerrillos Road, the fast-food strip outside Santa Fe where the City Different became the City Clone. Except for the green chile on the burgers, Cerrillos Road could have been anywhere in America and the same could be said for the motel. The cocktail party before the dinner was held in a large and anonymous room filled mostly with casually dressed booksellers. Awards were presented at this dinner for numerous categories of Western writing. The award for fiction was going to a well-known male writer whose macho cowboy heroes were more popular with women than they ought to be. Claire recognized him standing at the center of a group of women holding a glass of whiskey in his hand. From the waist down he was a cowboy in worn Levi's, scuffed boots and a leather belt with a silver buckle. From the waist up he was a city slicker in an expensive blazer, a white shirt and a red ascot looped under his chin. His upper body said "I'm a powerful dude." His lower body said "I'm a cowboy who doesn't care about this upper-body bullshit." Both were roles women found appealing, but a role women found truly irresistible was the drunken bad boy in need of a good woman to straighten him out. The writer played that one to the hilt, smoking, laughing, sipping the whiskey in his glass.

On her way to the bar to get herself a glass of wine Claire walked by his group and overheard him say, "I was getting ready to shoot that dude, but then I remembered that you can't smoke in prison." It wasn't hard to overhear him; the author had a boisterous voice followed by a hearty laugh. After he made this statement, he glanced around him to gauge the reaction of his audience, most of whom reacted exactly as he expected they would by laughing. He smiled benevolently, then happened to catch the eye of Claire, who wasn't smiling. The male author shrugged, grinned and tipped his glass.

While she waited at the bar for her glass of wine, Claire thought about his behavior. The cigarette, the glass, the humor, the outrageous statements, the bravado from a bottle reminded her of Ginny, but there was a level of detachment and irony in the author that she hadn't observed in Ginny. The way that he seemed to be standing apart and watching himself might indicate he was more intelligent than Ginny was or it might indicate that he was less drunk.

The author sat on the dais during dinner along with the MC and the other nominees. Claire sat at a round table with booksellers she knew. The food was the basic banquet dinner. The talk was familiar. Nothing at her own table required her full attention so she kept an eye on the male author during dinner, noticing that he rarely sipped at his drink, that after he finished eating he took a cigarette from a pack and tapped it against the table, but he never lit it. She often saw him studying the room with an amused detachment.

After dinner the MC, a bookseller unpracticed at the art of public speaking, stood up and began talking in an annoyingly deliberate voice. Five winners sat on the dais and all five of them were scheduled to speak, which would make for a long night. Claire wanted to hear the male author's speech — she was sure it would be entertaining — but she had something more important to do. She checked her watch. It was nine o'clock, a good time to ask one question for which she'd been seeking an answer.

She said good-bye to her bookseller friends and left the room, trying to draw as little attention to herself as possible. She walked outside, got into her car and drove toward the Plaza, turning right on Paseo de Peralta. At Acequia Madre, she turned right again, continuing on to Ginny's street. The adjacent houses were dark, but Ginny's house blazed like a planet alone in the sky.

Claire parked her car, walked to the door and rang the doorbell. Ginny could well be drunk and angry. She had some anxiety about confronting her alone at night, but felt it was something she had to do. When there was no response, Claire rang again. Eventually, she heard Ginny yell, "I'm coming. Okay? Goddamn it, I'm coming."

She unlocked the dead bolt, opened the door and blinked while her eyes adjusted to the darkness outside her house. Her dress was deeply wrinkled. Her hair had fallen into the tousled style known in Hollywood as bed head.

She squinted in Claire's direction. "Who's that?" she asked.

"It's me, Ginny."

"Who me?" Ginny replied.

"Claire Reynier."

Ginny rubbed her eyes with her knuckles. "Clairier," she said. "What are you doing here in the middle of the night?"

"It's not the middle of the night. It's nine-thirty."

"Nine-thirty? But it's so dark out there. It looks like the middle of the night." She wagged her finger at Claire. "Not good to be out alone at night. I never go outside after sunset. Come in." She slammed the door shut after Claire stepped inside and snapped the dead bolt into place.

"I was in town for a booksellers dinner," Claire said. "I thought I'd stop by and say hello."

"Hello," Ginny said, mimicking Claire. "Come in. Have a little drink with me."

Claire followed her down the hallway into

the living room and watched while Ginny collapsed on an overstuffed sofa. A half-full wineglass sat on the floor, but she had forgotten her offer to get Claire a drink. Just as well, Claire thought.

"I have DADS," Ginny whispered in a confessional tone. "Have you ever known anyone who has DADS?"

"What is it?" Claire asked.

"Deathly afraid of the dark or damn afraid of the dark. Take your pick." She fumbled with a pack of cigarettes. "I always had it. Even when I was little, I slept with the lights on, but it got really bad when I lived in Seattle. Our house was on an island. My husband was gone all the time — business, he said. It was always dark and gloomy. My melatonin is all fucked up, which is one reason why I moved here. I need the sunlight, artificial light, any kind of light. Everybody's afraid of something, aren't they?" She plucked a cigarette from the pack and lit it. "What is it you're afraid of? Tell me, Clairier."

"Dying alone," Claire replied. It was a legitimate fear, but not her greatest fear. At the moment her greatest fear was that she would be charged with murder.

"Everybody dies alone," Ginny said. "It's not the alone part. It's the dying part you've got to worry about."

"Did Evelyn Martin die alone?" Claire asked.

"No. She died in the company of whoever killed her."

"Was that you, Ginny?" Claire asked, leaning forward and trying to create a web of intimacy. Unlike Ginny she hadn't had the bar of her inhibitions lowered by alcohol. She had to jump a high hurdle of her reserve to ask this question, but she made herself do it.

"She was killed at night, wasn't she?" Ginny asked.

"Supposedly."

"It couldn't be me. I never go out after dark. I don't even go out at twilight because that would mean I have to come home after dark."

"But you had dinner with Elizabeth Best the night Evelyn was killed, didn't you?"

Ginny exhaled, flicked an ash from her cigarette, then dropped her voice to a conspiratorial whisper. "I can't stand Elizabeth Best. She's far too PC for me."

"But you told Detective Amaral you had dinner with her," Claire persisted.

"That was Elizabeth's idea. She said it would give both of us an alibi. I was home. She was with her boyfriend here, the blond guy. She didn't want that to come out because she has another boyfriend at home in Tucson. How does she do it?"

"She has a lot of energy," Claire said.

"I don't have any energy," Ginny said, putting her feet up on the sofa and resting her head on a pillow. "Lock the door when you leave," she mumbled before she fell asleep.

Claire made sure the cigarette was out, picked up the wineglass and the pack of cigarettes and carried them into the kitchen. Her own impulse would have been to turn the lamps off, but in deference to Ginny's phobia she left them burning. She wondered whether Ginny would recall this conversation in the morning. If she remembered it at all, she might remember it as a dream. Claire couldn't lock the dead bolt behind her without a key, but she made sure the knob in the door handle was locked. After she left the house, she tested it. There was enough ambient light in Santa Fe to block the view of the stars. When she looked up from Ginny's driveway all she could see was a murky glow.

But once she reached I-25, the sky became the ceiling of a vast black cave. A sliver of new moon hung over the Ortiz Mountains and Venus was a beauty mark below it. It made Claire glad all over again that she lived in New Mexico. Driving the state's empty highways created the illusion that the road belonged to her. For a few minutes she felt in control sitting in the cocoon of her truck listening to Mozart. But her serenity was shattered when she came across the lights of the state pen glaring in the east. She imagined what a cell there would look like and feel like — the total lack of privacy, the endless noise, the hostile inmates. The thought that she could end up spending time there made the cab of her truck feel less like a cocoon than a cage on wheels.

She should be leaving her defense to her cowboy lawyer, but she was having a hard time relinquishing control of her fate. There were ways in which her knowledge of the other suspects and her amateur status gave her investigation an advantage over Amaral's. Information elicited from a drunk would have no standing in court, but that didn't mean it wasn't accurate. In fact, Claire thought that statements made in unguarded moments were more likely to be truthful. Claire hoped she hadn't taken unfair advantage of an old friend and came to the conclusion that if she used this information to prove her own innocence she wouldn't be, but if she used it against Ginny she would.

She couldn't entirely eliminate Ginny and Elizabeth as suspects in her own mind, but she moved them to a back room. Elizabeth was with Brian. Ginny was afraid of the dark, unlikely to go out at night, and most likely would have been too inebriated to have pulled the murder off. That left Lynn, Miranda and their husbands in the parlor. If she was going to find evidence against any of them, she might have to use the same surreptitious means she had used with Elizabeth and Ginny. Was there any point in pursuing this if the information she elicited couldn't be used in court? Was her goal to prove her legal innocence or her moral innocence? She hoped that one might lead to the other.

When she got home, she went to her computer and composed a carefully worded e-mail to Miranda.

Recent events have made me think a lot about the past and our days at the U of A. I saw Elizabeth recently. I feel that I have changed and I imagine you feel the same way, too. But Elizabeth seems to have changed very little. She still has a nasty temper. I saw her treating her boyfriend's daughter badly, and I remember how horrible she was when she found you wearing her jacket and how angry that made you. I hope you are doing well on location, that the series will be a success and that I will get to see it on television.

Your old friend,
Claire

Chapter Fifteen

On Monday Claire had dinner with Celia at Olympia Café and went to a concert at Popejoy. After the concert she recalled there was a book in her office she had intended to take home with her, and she returned to pick it up. As she was leaving the center, she saw that Harrison was ahead of her. He walked through the door, turned left and continued down the hallway, presumably heading for the lot behind the library where the staff parked their vehicles. She stayed a respectful distance behind, not following him exactly since they were both going in the same direction. Yet the fact that it was night and no one else happened to be in the hallway gave her the sensation that she was a hunter stalking a prey. If she intended to confront him about his dissertation, this could be the moment. He walked past the bookstore and an exhibit of photographs on the opposite wall and went out the door. She followed him down the sidewalk, listening to the sound of her own footsteps and wondering if he heard them, wondering if he suspected that he was being followed. He might imagine that someone wanted to confront him or even rob him, but she doubted it would occur to him that anyone had the power to cast doubt on words he had written years ago. He never turned around, just kept on walking toward the parking lot at a measured pace. He seemed tired to Claire, which added to his vulnerability. When he got to the lot, he clicked the remote that unlocked the door of his SUV. Claire approached as he put his hand on the door.

"Good evening, Harrison," she said.

He spun around. "Claire. I didn't know you were behind me."

"I came back to my office to pick up a book," she replied. "Were you working late?"

"Yes." He paused. They were alone in the parking lot after dark. It was a perfect time for confidences if there were ever going to be any. He cleared his throat. "Is there anything new in the murder investigation?" he asked.

"Not really," Claire replied, wishing he hadn't used the word *murder*.

"I don't suppose your copy of *The Confidence-Man* has turned up?" His expression was covetous. His long white fingers clutched the door handle.

"Not to my knowledge."

"What will become of the one that was

found in your office?"

"I don't know."

"You're quite convinced the signature in that book is fraudulent?"

"I believe it is a fraud, but it would take an expert to prove it one way or the other."

"There are very few signed copies of *The Confidence-Man* and they are expensive."

"That's another reason I think the signature was forged. It would be far easier and cheaper to find an unsigned copy and fake the signature than it would be to locate a signed copy. You told me you did your dissertation on Herman Melville, didn't you?" That sentence made its way from the back of her mind to the tip of her tongue and slipped out without any conscious effort on her part.

"Yes," he replied, opening the door to his vehicle.

If Claire intended to speak, this was the moment, but what would she say? I've discovered that you plagiarized parts of your dissertation, and I can prove it? That sentence did not roll off her tongue.

"I'll see you tomorrow," Harrison said.

"Good night," Claire replied.

She drove home wondering whether her failure to mention the plagiarism should be considered wisdom, kindness or cowardice. As she turned into her subdivision she saw the Sandias silhouetted against the sky and was reminded of how wild the mountains became at night. It was too late to let Nemesis out. He protested by meowing and rubbing against her legs. Trying to ignore him, she went to her office, picked up the Oxford World's Classics edition and replayed the conversation with Harrison, wondering all over again who had placed the copy of *The Confidence-Man* in her office. Any of the suspects could have located a copy of that book, forged Melville's signature and put it on her shelf. Claire believed she had accounted for Ginny and Elizabeth's whereabouts on the night in question. If neither one of them had killed Evelyn, then neither one of them had a motive to frame her. As for the other alibis, she had Lynn's word that she had been at home with Steve, Miranda's word that she had been on location. Apparently Amaral believed them, but maybe his investigation hadn't gone far enough.

She checked her e-mail before going to bed, looking for an answer from Miranda but not finding one. It didn't arrive until three days later.

"Hi Claire," it began.

Sorry it took so long to get back to you. Still muy busy here. The show is going well. Is that detective ready to charge anyone with the death of Evelyn Martin? It won't be you, I hope. Of course I remember how horrible Elizabeth was about the jacket. You're right. I was furious and I wanted to strangle her, but I got over it. As time went by, I bore her no grudge. I hope all is well with you. Stay in touch.

Miranda

Claire turned off her computer feeling that a fish had flopped onto her desk. In a way, her earlier e-mail to Miranda had been a fishing expedition. She went through her mental album of the U of A days but found no photo there of a very angry Miranda. The Miranda she remembered from the incident with Elizabeth remained evasive, not confrontational. The recollection in this e-mail was not Claire's recollection. It would be interesting to investigate what that meant, but Erwin seemed to consider himself the guardian at Miranda's gate. Wondering if there was any way to get around him, she called Lynn in Cave Creek.

"How are you doing?" Lynn asked. "Anything new on the investigation?"

"Not really," Claire replied. "I had another e-mail from Miranda. Have you talked to her recently?"

"Not recently."

"Do you have her phone number in Mexico by any chance?"

"No."

"Have you seen Erwin?"

"He was here a couple of days ago. He asked about you, how you were doing, whether you were still under investigation."

"What did you say?"

"I didn't know how the investigation was going, but I thought you were fine."

"How did Erwin know I was under investigation?"

"Steve told him. *Are* you still under investigation?" Lynn asked in a hesitant voice.

"Yes," Claire admitted. "In fact I've hired a lawyer."

"I'm sorry to hear that."

The conversation moved on to other things. Claire got off the phone as soon as possible and called Erwin.

"Erwin, this is Claire Reynier."

"Oh, yes, of course, Claire Reynier, and how are you?" The gruffness in his voice seemed to have been smoothed by oil.

"All right, and you?"

"Very well, thank you."

"Lynn said you'd been asking about me?"

"Nothing special. Just wondering how you were."

"I'd like to talk to Miranda. I was wondering if you could give me her number. Is she still on location in Mexico?"

"Still in Mexico. In fact, I am going down there this weekend to see her. She's so busy it's hard for her to talk on the phone. Why don't I have her call you? Let me have your number at work just in case she gets a break and finds it easier to call in the daytime."

Asking for her work number struck Claire as the kind of fine detail a liar would use as a diversionary tactic. She didn't really expect Miranda to call her at work or at home, but she gave Erwin the number.

Sid Hyland's secretary called Claire on Friday morning. "Could you come into the office this afternoon?" she asked. "Sid wants to talk to you."

"What about?" Claire asked.

"You'll have to ask him," the secretary replied.

On her way to Sid Hyland's office, Claire got stuck in traffic on Central, and her feeling of apprehension increased by the minute. Trying to get through the canyon of downtown was stop, go, stop. She was stuck behind a van and couldn't see far enough ahead to find the cause of the problem. At one long delay, she found herself sitting opposite a woman in a car heading east. The woman stared straight ahead, and Claire had nothing else to do but study her. They were approximately the same age. The woman's hair had been frosted blond. Her face was tense. The unforgiving New Mexico sun showed the lines in her neck and the sags beneath her chin. Claire wondered if that was what she looked like when she didn't put on a face for the mirror. Frustrated? Worried? After fifty did women turn into clones, indistinguishable from one another? Her future depended on being able to differentiate herself from a woman who superficially resembled her. Sitting opposite a stranger who fell into the same category didn't give her much hope. The traffic lurched forward, and she drove past the woman, never discovering if they had something in common or nothing.

Although she had left early, she got to Hyland's office late and found him standing behind his desk. She tried to judge what this meeting was about from his manner. Her first impression was that he didn't seem to be as invincibly confident as he had on their previous meeting.

"Have a seat," he said, waving his hand in the direction of a chair and sitting down himself.

"What is this about?" she asked.

Hyland leaned back, brushed the hair from his collar and paused, seemingly for effect. Claire supposed that was a litigator's prerogative.

"Amaral found the murder weapon," he said.

Claire felt relieved, thinking that was bound to exonerate her. "What is it?" she asked.

"A cast-iron frying pan."

"I'm not surprised it was something from the kitchen. Where was it found?"

"A member of a road crew working on the southbound side of I-25 found it inside a plastic trash bag, apparently tossed from a vehicle. It was a huge break for the police. It could have taken years for anyone to locate the bag in that area, if it was ever found at all."

Hyland didn't need to remind Claire that a person driving from Santa Fe to Albuquerque would be in the southbound lane. But then so would a person heading from Santa Fe to Arizona.

"He found a set of partial prints on the

frying pan that matched Evelyn Martin's and another set that he hasn't been able to identify yet."

Claire had never owned a cast-iron frying pan so she knew the prints couldn't be hers.

"The blood on the frying pan matched the victim's." Hyland leaned forward, placed his forearms on the desk and focused his attention on Claire. "There's one more thing. The frying pan was wrapped in a pink towel. Hair and blood samples found on the towel match those of the victim. The towel was embroidered with the initials CRB."

"Oh, God," Claire said, feeling that her own head had just come in contact with something hard and unyielding.

"Do you own such a towel?" Hyland asked.

"Yes, and my married name was Burch. I received a set of embroidered towels as a gift from my husband's mother when we were still married. I used them in the guest bathroom. Evelyn must have stolen one when she stayed at my house. If she took it from the linen closet, I wouldn't have noticed."

"Apparently the towel was used to mop up the victim's blood or possibly in an attempt to wipe fingerprints from the murder weapon."

"Or to implicate me if the weapon were ever found."

"That's possible," Hyland agreed.

"If I went to Evelyn's house to kill her, would I have taken my own towel?"

"Unlikely, but you might have found your towel there and thought it wise to dispose of it. I'm not saying that's what happened, only that's how a prosecutor could see it. Human motivation is murky, but fingerprints don't lie." Hyland paused again. "Prints taken from the book that Amaral found in your office also match those of the victim. He wants to fingerprint you."

"My fingerprints won't be on that book, but they could be on something else Evelyn took from my house. Do I have to agree?"

"Only when Amaral gets a court order, which he is sure to do."

"If I offer to be fingerprinted, would that make me appear more cooperative and less guilty?"

"It might," Hyland said. "But I prefer to make the police do the work."

"It will mean more waiting on my part."

"Waiting can work for you, if you don't let it get to you. It's always possible exculpatory evidence will turn up in the meantime. My advice would be to take the weekend off and try to think about something else."

"I'll try."

Hyland stood up. "I'll be in touch," he said.

Claire stood up, too, and looked into his eyes, trying to read whether or not he believed she was guilty. She suspected that he didn't care. What mattered to Sid Hyland was what he could prove, and there she began to see doubt.

Chapter Sixteen

When Claire got home she went to the linen closet immediately and counted the towels with the initials CRB embroidered on them. It was a compulsive act, she knew, since it was already obvious that Evelyn had stolen one from her house. She found eight bath towels and seven hand towels in the closet. Having Amaral find the murder weapon wrapped in the missing towel and knowing that the prints on *The Confidence-Man* found in her office matched the victim's made her feel that someone was pulling her strings. Having Amaral ask for her fingerprints made Claire feel that the strings had been jerked tight.

It took a long time to fall asleep. Claire woke up in the middle of the night with confidence men and women on her mind. The next time she woke up, darkness indicated it was still night, but the numbers on her clock read five-thirty — early morning. She felt a need to get out of the house and take a long drive to clear her head. She had planned to work on a publish-or-perish article over the weekend, but she could take her tape recorder along and dictate her thoughts as she drove. The urge to be on the highway was so strong she skipped tai chi, had a cup of coffee and put out some food for the cat. It was a cold, windy morning, so she put on her windbreaker before she went out the door.

When she backed out of her garage, she saw the sun cracking open the sky behind the Sandias with a yellow light. It was always better to keep one's back to the sun when driving. West was Claire's preferred direction anyway; east led to Texas, west led to Arizona, where she might find the answers to some oppressive questions. She took Paseo del Norte across the Rio Grande, turned south on Coors and headed west on I-40. When she reached the top of the West Mesa, she glanced in her rearview mirror and saw that the sun had risen to a point where it appeared to be sitting on top of the Sandias.

Eighty miles later she stopped at the Stuckey's exit, had another cup of coffee, then turned south onto Highway 117, which passed through El Malpais National Monument where the red cliffs were marked by the striations of weather and time. It was a part of New Mexico that Claire loved, and she had come here before when searching for the answer to a question. She clicked on her tape recorder, but instead of recording her thoughts about collection development at CSWR, she began recording her thoughts about Evelyn Martin. The tape recorder whirred as it listened. It didn't measure up to talking to an old friend, but until Claire had figured out what role her old friends had played, she was no longer comfortable talking to them.

It was only nine-thirty when she came to the town of Quemado, and she still had most of the day ahead of her. She turned west on Route 60, one of the most open of New Mexico's open highways. When she reached the Arizona border, she crossed it. There was no interstate here and this part of Arizona was crisscrossed with state highways that mirrored the lay of the land. From the air the roads looked as serpentine as rivers and canyons. Driving them was a challenge that required full concentration, so Claire clicked off the tape recorder and put it in the pocket of her windbreaker. She abandoned Route 60 for Route 260 at Show Low, climbed the Mogollon Rim and entered a forest of ponderosa pine. At Payson she turned north on a meandering road that eventually came out on Interstate 17 at Camp Verde. From here it was eighty miles south to New River. A series of choices or an inner compass had led her near the town where Miranda lived when she was not on location.

She drove south on I-17 and got off at the New River exit. The citizens here were about to lose control of their town. Soon there would be a huge planned community at this exit, but for now it was as rural as Cave Creek had been when Lynn moved there twenty-five years ago. The desert here was unexpectedly green. Claire loved the vegetation — the saguaro, the prickly pear, the ocotillo and the teddy bear cholla, a plant that always appeared to be backlit. In Phoenix the desert had been reduced to landscaping, but here it was a force. She found it interesting to contemplate where people who could live anywhere — people who had money or whose jobs didn't tie them to a specific locale, people who could turn their houses into islands — chose to live. This was a town Claire might have chosen herself if she hadn't had to work or to live alone. The desert here offered more than warmth or sunshine. It offered a wild and rare beauty.

She stopped at a Fina station to ask for directions to 203 Javelina Lane, the address she had found for Miranda Kohl and Erwin Bush. The directions involved numerous turns on unmarked dirt roads and were complicated enough that Claire wrote them down. The houses were low, nearly hidden by the vegetation, and separated by acres of green. The area was a mix of small houses, trailers and large houses. The lack of landmarks gave Claire the sensation she was negotiating a maze and that the deeper she immersed herself, the harder it would be to find the way out.

She hoped there was some truth at least to Erwin's statement that he would be away for the weekend. He might have been lying about going to Mexico, but it would be far better for her if he had gone somewhere. A coyote ran out in front of Claire, chasing something she couldn't see and so intent on the chase that it paid no attention to her truck. The path she took kept bringing her closer to Apache Peak. She came to another unmarked road, glanced at the directions she had written down and took a left. A half mile later she saw a stone at the edge of a driveway with Miranda's number painted on it. No dwelling was visible from the road, but if there was a driveway there had to be a house.

Claire began to wish she had a rifle balanced across her rear window or had brought a bodyguard. This was a very lonely place to be confronting a possible murderer. Her premise for some time had been that Evelyn's death was either accidental or self-defense, that someone had confronted Evelyn with the truth, that Evelyn had attacked and the murderer had fought back. She had come to that conclusion by putting herself in the murderer's shoes, easy enough to do once she became a suspect. As she continued down the driveway, she had to consider the possibility the murder had been committed with intent. If that were the case, what was to stop a person who had killed once from killing again? The driveway was barely wider than Claire's truck and surrounded by thorny vegetation that made it impossible to turn around. There was no choice but to continue. She was almost relieved when she reached the house and it appeared that no one was home.

The doors were all shut. No dogs barked or ran out to greet her. She stepped out of the truck and the sound of the door closing behind her fractured the silence. The house had been designed to blend into its site with the skill of a Frank Lloyd Wright building. There was no landscaping. The desert came right up to the door. It was close to the ground and the exterior had been stained subtle desert colors. At first glance it appeared as modest as a bungalow, but that was deceiving. It was actually a very large house that sprawled like a centipede across the desert. It was totally isolated — a place one could live for years and have no contact with neighbors.

Sometimes when Claire tried to evaluate how well she was doing vis-à-vis an old friend, she would compare their living situations. This was a place she would have taken in a minute for the beauty of the setting and the subtlety of the architecture. It made her own house seem like a tract house. If Miranda was referring to this house when she said she had been doing well, she'd been correct.

Claire went to the front door and rang a brass bell shaped like a lizard. She heard a melodious ring deep within the house, but it was not followed by anyone calling out "I'm coming" or by the pad of footsteps. She waited a few minutes, rang again and heard nothing but silence. She walked to the garage, which had a side window, and peered in. There was room for three cars, but the garage was empty, which gave her the confidence to circle the house. She could always say she was looking to see if anyone was at the pool if an owner showed up. Claire followed a path around the house expecting to come to a pool, and eventually she found one surrounded by a patio with weathered wood furniture, pink umbrellas and pots of flowering plants. It was what she thought of as an infinity pool; the water appeared to drop off the edge and disappear. An empty glass sat on a poolside table, the first sign that anyone was in residence.

"Hello," Claire called, but there was no answer.

She climbed onto the patio and walked up to the house. Most of the windows were on this side facing toward the mountains and away from the sun. At first Claire could see nothing but reflections in the tinted glass, which had a sort of bronze glow that made her own reflection appear to be a gilded statue. She had to get close to the glass in order to see through it. It was hard to tell exactly what purpose the room she saw served in the scheme of a very large house, but it was beautiful and elegant enough to give Claire a tinge of envy. The ceiling was high, but not overwhelming. The room was beautifully proportioned and furnished in a subtle style she admired. The tile around the fireplace had ghostly figures that resembled petroglyphs. It was a room with soft colors, a room that whispered. This wasn't an outside house like the Grangers', but an indoor house that encouraged fantasy.

Claire wondered why Lynn hadn't told her how exquisite Miranda's house was. For a moment she wondered if she could even have gotten the wrong house, but then she remembered how inattentive Lynn was to decoration. This house reflected the Miranda she had known — imaginative, creative, beautiful. If it inspired a bit of envy in her, it could have caused devouring envy in the unstable Evelyn. Of course there was no indication that Evelyn had ever been here. Or perhaps she should revise that to Erwin had implied she had never been here. A raven cawed, broke the silence, then flew over the roof and dive-bombed the patio.

Claire moved on, following the path around the other side of the house and peering through windows as she went. Unlike Evelyn's bare-boned rental house, every room in this house showed signs of Miranda's exquisite taste, although little sign of Miranda. Claire saw books and artwork, but all the clothes or objects she spotted appeared to be Erwin's. In the largest bedroom the bed was unmade, and a man's khaki pants and Topsiders lay on the floor. The master bath had a Jacuzzi with a skylight above it for watching the stars and the moon. Towels were wadded up and

235

tossed on the floor. The kitchen had an open bag of chips and a half-finished Corona on the counter.

Claire came to a library with shelves full of books, a fireplace and a chaise lounge with a reading lamp on an end table beside it. She was able to read the titles of the books on the end table and saw nonfiction adventure stories by John Krakauer and Sebastian Junger. She loved libraries and this one was a classic. The fireplace — an extravagance in Arizona — had silhouettes of Mayan faces in the tile. The wrought-iron tools were black with brass handles and as well designed and carefully chosen as everything else in the house.

Claire followed the path that eventually led back to the front of the building. When she reached her truck she stood still for a minute wondering whether she should wait for someone to come home or move on. The lengthening shadows said she needed to think about where she would spend the night. She knew there was a room available for her at Lynn's, but should she take advantage of it?

Her reverie was punctuated by the sound of a horse's hooves pounding the driveway. There were no stables on the property and she hadn't seen any sign that anyone here had a horse. As the animal got closer, the sound intensified until she began to imagine the cavalry would gallop over the horizon. When it finally appeared, it was only one horse ridden by one woman with long blond hair wearing jeans and riding boots. She reined in the horse but remained seated in the saddle, towering over Claire.

"Hello?" she asked, turning her greeting into a question.

"Hello," Claire replied. "I'm Claire Reynier, an old friend of Miranda Kohl's. I happened to be in town, and I stopped by to visit."

"Jerry Bartlett," the woman said, bending down and extending her hand. Her long blond hair and her posture on the horse made Jerry seem youthful, but her skin sent the message that she had spent years in the sun. "Miranda's out of town, and so is Erwin. He asked me to look after the place while he's away."

"It's the first time I've been here. It's a beautiful house."

"It is," Jerry agreed.

"Do you live nearby?"

"A couple of miles down the road." In New River that could put her in a trailer or an equally beautiful house.

"Did Erwin and Miranda take a trip together?" Claire asked, trying to elicit some useful information from Jerry.

"It's been years since Erwin and Miranda did anything together," she scoffed. "She left him about a month ago."

"Are you sure?"

"That's what Erwin told me."

"Where did she go?"

"Who knows? With the residuals she gets from the commercials and the TV cameos she does, she could live anywhere. No matter where actresses have houses, their real homes remain in New York and LA. This is a vacation house for her. Erwin's the one who takes care of it."

"I thought that Miranda was filming a TV series in Mexico."

"That's the first I've heard of it," Jerry replied. "What part would there be for a woman in her fifties? The mother? Can you imagine Miranda playing a mother day after day? Miranda wouldn't want to be anyone day after day, certainly not a mother. Besides, a series is very hard work and she doesn't want to work that hard. She makes commercials and does guest appearances on TV shows. Most of the time she travels and does whatever she wants to do."

Claire watched the shadow of Jerry and her horse stretch across the ground. The raven that seemed to haunt the property flew over and cawed again.

"I need to check the house and make sure everything is all right," Jerry said. "I'll tell Erwin you were here."

Claire thought it might be better if Erwin didn't know she'd been here, but her response was, "All right. Do you know where he is or when he'll be back?"

"He's in Mexico for a week. See you," Jerry said, clicking to her horse and heading for the path that circled the house.

"Good-bye," Claire replied.

There was nothing to do now but turn her truck around and head out the driveway. Since she couldn't do any more investigating with Jerry on the property, she decided to retrace her path through the maze of New River, go to Cave Creek and spend the night with Lynn.

Chapter Seventeen

As Claire started her truck she pushed the button to clear the odometer, intending to keep track of the mileage between Miranda's house and the Grangers'. It ended up taking her forty minutes to cover twenty miles. As she neared Cave Creek, the growing number of houses beside the road made her feel she'd been covering decades as well as miles. In terms of density New River looked today as Cave Creek did twenty-five years ago. Ten years from now Cave Creek would be Scottsdale. New River would be Cave Creek and some town farther out would become New River. Claire knew that people who contributed to an area's growth when they moved in didn't have the right to complain about further growth. It was no longer an issue in Albuquerque, where anyone who claimed the right to keep the city from expanding had long since given up, but it was still an issue north of Phoenix. The fact that Lynn had lived in Cave Creek for twenty-five years might give her the right to complain, but she never heard Lynn complain about anything. It wasn't her nature. As she negotiated the roads, she wondered how often

Lynn or Steve or Miranda had made this trip. Erwin seemed to be the one who acted as messenger between the two houses. When she reached the Grangers' and pulled into the driveway Lynn and Steve were sitting on the patio. They stood up when they recognized the truck and walked over to greet her.

"Claire?" Lynn asked. "What on earth are you doing here?" She pressed her hand to her forehead. "Don't tell me you said you were coming and I forgot."

Steve hovered behind Lynn like a shadow while Claire hugged her friend.

"No, you didn't forget," Claire said. "To come here was a spur-of-the-moment decision. Amaral found the murder weapon in a trash bag beside the southbound lane of I-25. It was a cast-iron frying pan."

"That figures," Lynn said. Steve said nothing.

"It was wrapped in a monogrammed towel that Evelyn had stolen from my house. Amaral wants to fingerprint me."

"Oh, God," Lynn said.

"It left me feeling overwhelmed. I got in the car this morning and just drove. I ended up here."

"You're always welcome at our house," Lynn said. She wasn't a person to doubt a friend no matter what the evidence indicated. Her hug was as comforting as a pillow, but when Claire looked across her shoulder, she saw skepticism in Steve's gray eyes.

She stepped away from Lynn. "I went the back way through Payson and came out on I-17 at Camp Verde. I stopped at Miranda's on my way here."

"Was she home?" Lynn asked.

"No. Neither was Erwin, but a woman named Jerry Bartlett rode up on her horse. She said she was checking the house while Erwin was away." Her instinct told her to give the rest of the information to Lynn when Steve wasn't in the background. "Do you know Jerry?" she asked. "A woman with long blond hair?"

"No," Lynn replied.

Steve's eyes darted away, suggesting he knew more about Jerry than his wife.

"You didn't tell me that Miranda lived in such a beautiful house."

"Didn't I?" Lynn asked. "It is beautiful, but we don't go there very often. Miranda values her quiet time when she is in Arizona. I understand that. It's one reason we've remained friends for so long."

"Can I get you something to drink?" Steve asked.

"A glass of wine," Claire said.

"You got it." Steve headed for the house.

"Let's sit on the patio," Lynn said. "Or are you tired of sitting by now?"

"No. I got out of the truck and walked around when I was at Miranda's."

They went over to the patio. Civil twilight was approaching, but it hadn't arrived yet. Claire couldn't help comparing the simplicity of the Grangers' house to the elegance of Miranda's. The Grangers were comfortable. Miranda went way beyond comfortable.

Having been married many years herself, Claire knew that spouses might react in one way if you presented them with information when they were together and another when they were apart. "Did you know that Miranda and Erwin had separated?" she asked, taking advantage of Steve's absence.

"No!" Lynn responded, putting her hand on the back of a chair to steady herself and appearing genuinely shocked. "Why on earth do you think that?"

"Jerry Bartlett told me that Miranda moved out about a month ago, and she thought she might have gone to LA or New York."

"Miranda never said anything to me."

"Have you talked to her in the last month?"

"I don't know that I actually talked to her, but she's been e-mailing me. Not as often as she used to, but I figured she was busy with the new show. I can't imagine that Miranda would leave Erwin without telling me." She seemed to deflate as she sank into the patio chair.

Seeing how upset her friend was, Claire touched her shoulder and said, "Maybe she hasn't had the right moment yet."

"Maybe. What are you going to do about Amaral?" she asked, changing the subject.

"I don't know. If he gets a court order — and I'm sure he will — I'll have to be finger-printed. It might be better to volunteer. I'll make a decision when I get home."

Steve came back with the drinks and the conversation moved on to the weather, the back roads of Arizona, the coyote Claire saw running down the road in New River. Eventually Steve got up to prepare dinner. Claire waited a few minutes, then said she had to use the bathroom.

She found him in the kitchen standing over a cutting board, inserting a knife between the skin and the breast of a piece of chicken. He began to cut the skin loose, an act that required a very sharp knife.

"No more Kentucky Fried Chicken for me," he said.

Claire felt she had little time to circle the issue so she got right to the point. "What can you tell me about Jerry Bartlett?" she asked.

Steve continued cutting until he'd removed the skin. He dropped it into the trash, then turned to look at Claire. "I know she is a friend of Erwin's," he admitted.

"How good a friend?"

The gray eyes got cloudy as he debated how much of a friend's confidence he was willing to reveal. "It's possible they are having an affair. Erwin hinted that they were, but you've met Erwin. Sometimes he implies more than there is."

"Did he tell you that Miranda had left him?" Claire asked.

Steve picked up the knife and began working on the chicken breast again, carving the meat away from the bone. "He said something about it," he replied without looking up.

"When?"

"I don't remember exactly. A couple of weeks ago."

"Why didn't anybody tell Lynn?"

"I can't speak for Erwin, but speaking for myself, I knew she'd be hurt that Miranda hadn't told her. You must have noticed that Lynn places Miranda on a pedestal.

Miranda has an interesting career. Lynn has me." He put down the knife, touched his heart and gave Claire a wry grin. "Or what's left of me. Lynn thinks Miranda is her close friend, but Miranda is a butterfly. She's here, she's there. Even when she is here, we hardly ever see her. An actress's life is far more exciting than our domestic life. They belong to their audiences, their agents, their producers, not to their friends or their mates."

"Do you know where Erwin went?"

"He told me he was going to Mexico to look at a property in Baja."

It was clear that he considered the kitchen his domain. Nevertheless, Claire felt an obligation to offer to help. He declined and she went to the bathroom then back out to the patio.

When dinner was ready, Steve called them to the table. The food was fat-free and the conversation was also on the lean side. Claire could only give it one half of her mind while the other replayed the events of the last few days.

They went to bed early. Claire listened for the yip of the coyotes, but for reasons known only to them, they were silent. When she finally fell asleep, she had dreams in which a part of her seemed to be standing outside the action crying "Get me out of this." In one dream she saw her own over-sized fingerprints stamped in black ink in Evelyn Martin's house. In another she saw Evelyn's decomposed body sprawled across the kitchen floor, the rotting flesh, the turquoise dress, the bleached hair. As she watched, it seemed to inflate like a grotesque balloon. She woke from this dream wondering how anyone even knew that the inflated body was Evelyn Martin. Because you said so, she thought before she fell asleep again. You identified the hair.

The next time she woke up it was still dark, but she could tell that morning was coming by the sound of the chattering birds. As she lay in bed and waited for the cold light of dawn, she revised her dreams and reminded herself that she had not been the one who identified Evelyn Martin. The Santa Fe police identified her by checking dental records. She got out of bed and got dressed. The door was closed to Steve and Lynn's bedroom, and the house was quiet. Claire let herself out the front door and walked down the road until she came to a dry streambed, a place she and Lynn had walked before. She followed the stream, which had carved a deep and sandy path.

There were no houses or people visible from the depths of the arroyo. She enjoyed the morning freshness and looked for tracks. She didn't see the chevron pattern of rattlesnake skin, but she did see the swirls of lizard tails and the footprints that formed dots beside them. A raven flew over and cawed. For all she knew it was the same raven she had seen at Miranda's house.

She kept on following the streambed through the narrow canyon knowing it would eventually lead to Cave Creek; water always sought the lowest level. As she walked, studying the ground, thinking about tracks and signs, the thought came to her that a sign that seemed so obvious had been misinterpreted. The idea was so startling that it took a while to absorb it, but once she opened this door, other questions appeared and other answers. She kept on walking and thinking, wondering what she could do to correct the error if there had been one.

The sound of running water interrupted her reverie and she knew that Cave Creek was around the bend. It was one of those rare streams in Arizona that actually had water in it. As far as Claire knew, it flowed year-round fed by springs and snowfall from the mountains. She stood next to the stream watching the amber water flow, enjoying the ripples and shadows and the refreshing sound of the running water. She felt the sun on her back and realized that Steve and Lynn would be up by now and wondering where she was. She turned and followed the arroyo back to the house, picking up her pace and starting to sweat even though it was still early morning. As she came around a bend, she saw Steve rushing toward her.

"Claire," he called. "I was hoping these were your footsteps. Lynn got worried when she didn't find you in the house."

"I'm sorry," Claire replied. "I woke up early and went for a walk. I didn't think anyone would miss me."

"Since I had the heart attack, Lynn worries about everything. Then Evelyn was murdered and you all became suspects. When Lynn worries she eats. She's probably sitting in the garage right now with a bag of potato chips. Maybe that's why she sent me to look for you, so she could eat. For every pound I lose, she gains five."

"You know about the eating?"

"How else would she be putting on so much weight? But if you tell her I know, it'll just upset her."

As they walked toward the house, Claire thought about the secrets couples kept from each other. Secrets could be helpful or they could be destructive, depending on the size and the subject of the secret. Since Steve already knew about Lynn's eating, she saw no harm in asking if he also knew that Evelyn had stolen Lynn's cache of food.

"I knew," he told her. "But I didn't say anything to Lynn."

"Did Erwin tell you?"

"Yes," Steve said.

"So that means Lynn told Miranda, Miranda told Erwin, Erwin told you. If you told Lynn it would complete the circle."

"I know." Steve continued walking at a rapid pace, keeping his eyes on the ground. The tracks were still embedded in the sand, but Claire suspected he was going too fast to notice them.

If Lynn had been eating while she waited, she'd hidden the signs. She was standing in the driveway holding a coffee mug.

"I was worried about you," she said, giving Claire a hug.

"I'm sorry," Claire replied. "I woke up early and went for a walk. I followed the streambed to Cave Creek. You and I have been there before."

"I don't go there so early in the morning when the rattlesnakes are still out."

Claire thought how people who were

looking for a comfortable life were drawn to the desert by the warmth and the sun, but it remained a thorny and dangerous place. It was one of the things she liked about it. Awareness of danger sharpened the senses, which was not a bad thing. "There's good visibility in the streambed. I watched for rattlesnake tracks, and I didn't see any," she said.

"I know you've lived in the desert and you know your way around. I'm sorry to be such a worrywart, but so many things have happened lately. It makes me uncomfortable."

Claire felt she was standing outside a rectangle formed by the two couples — Steve and Lynn, Erwin and Miranda. She couldn't say any more about the food theft without revealing that Steve knew about the eating and upsetting the balance. But she felt she could question Lynn about the past and her memory of Miranda. She waited until Steve went into the house.

"The last time Miranda and I e-mailed each other I mentioned the incident at the U of A when Elizabeth found her wearing the jacket. What do you remember about it?"

"That Elizabeth was a bitch."

"Do you remember what Miranda's reaction was? Did she blow up at Elizabeth?"

"No. Miranda wasn't a confrontational

person. I think she was more puzzled and hurt than angry."

They went inside to get away from the sun, and Claire asked if she could use their computer to check her e-mail. Although Steve was the cook in this house, in other ways the Grangers followed traditional roles. He was the brain, Lynn was the heart. She took care of the quail, he took care of the computer. Steve led her into his office, logged on to the Internet, and left Claire alone. Taking her first step on the road toward answering her questions, she went to AOL's web site, the one with which she was familiar. She did a people search of the white pages and found a J. Bartlett listed in New River. Jerry, presumably. An initial in the phone book usually meant a woman trying to conceal the fact. It wouldn't fool many people, but it was better that people didn't know your name if they wanted to cause you trouble. Claire printed out a map from I-17 to Jerry's residence, then searched the yellow pages. If she were searching Phoenix her task would have been impossible, but in New River there was only one entry in the category she searched. Then, if only because she'd said she intended to, she checked her e-mail to find the usual collection of unsolicited credit card offers and porn.

After lunch Claire said she needed to get going so she wouldn't have to spend much time driving home after dark. Lynn protested, but not very hard. Steve didn't protest at all. Claire got in her truck and found her way to I-17, but instead of turning north toward home, she turned south toward Phoenix. She got off near downtown, found herself an anonymous motel and checked in. She spent the rest of the afternoon at the Heard Museum, had dinner at a restaurant she liked, went back to the motel and went to bed early. In the morning she called CSWR and left a message that she wouldn't be in. She dressed and combed her hair but put on no makeup, which left her looking appropriately wan. She had a bagel and a cup of coffee, then got in her truck and negotiated the rush-hour traffic through Phoenix to New River.

The address she had wasn't far from the interstate. It was the office of a dentist named Charles Rule. Dr. Rule might be able to answer her question, but to get to see a busy dentist could require a performance equal to any of Miranda's. Claire had once had a toothache and had a vivid memory of the intense pain. She would have to call on memory since she had little experience as an actress. She parked her truck and went into the office, where she encountered a receptionist wearing a pink smock and a name tag that read Silvia.

"May I help you?" she asked.

Claire took a deep breath then said, "I have a terrible toothache. I think the root may be dying. I don't have an appointment, but I was wondering if the dentist could see me. I'm visiting a friend here in town and I can't get myself back home in this kind of pain."

"We should be able to fit you in," Silvia said, handing her a form to fill out.

"Thanks," Claire said. "This is a small town. You might know my friend here, Miranda Kohl."

"Oh, yes," Silvia said. "She's a patient of ours and so is her husband. Have a seat. Dr. Rule will be with you as soon as possible."

Claire sat down in the reception area and flipped through a magazine, sucking on her cheek and trying to keep up the appearance of being in physical pain. The mental and emotional discomfort she felt was real enough. She didn't like being an impostor, but she only needed to be one long enough to get herself into the dentist's office. She waited an hour before Dr. Rule was able to see her. Silvia led Claire down the hall to the examining room.

Claire lay back in the reclining seat, stared at photographs of clouds on the ceiling and listened to New Age music while she waited for Dr. Rule.

"Howdy," he said when he entered the room.

"Hello," replied Claire, sitting up in the chair.

Dr. Rule was a tall, middle-aged man with a bald head and intelligent green eyes that expressed a keen interest in her. Perhaps because she was a new patient. She doubted he could be very interested in another root canal or toothache.

"What seems to be the problem?" he asked.

Claire straightened her back, squared her shoulders and said, "I have a confession to make. I don't have a toothache."

"Oh?" asked Dr. Rule, raising an eyebrow. "Then why are you here?"

"I'm an old friend of Miranda Kohl's. Your receptionist told me you're her dentist."

"I am, but if you're a friend of Miranda's, shouldn't she have told you that herself?" He stepped away from Claire, leading her to think there was a patient/dentist confidentiality he didn't want to violate.

"She should, but I can't find Miranda and

I'm concerned about her."

"She travels a lot."

"I know, but this is different."

"What makes you think I'll be able to find her? We see Miranda twice a year for cleaning. She rarely needs any dental work."

"I'm not expecting you to find her. I want you to see if you have her x-rays."

Dr. Rule cocked his head. "Of course I have her x-rays. Why wouldn't I?"

"A woman that Miranda and I went to college with was found dead several weeks ago in her house in Santa Fe. The woman lived alone, the body was badly decomposed and was identified through dental records. Evidence has come out that years ago this woman robbed her friends and framed Miranda. I'm beginning to think Miranda went to her house intending to confront her and ended up dead. If the body found in that house is Miranda's, one way to prove it would be through your dental records."

"Are you saying you think Miranda was murdered?"

"I am afraid that's what happened."

"That would be horrible." Dr. Rule put his hand to his cheek and stepped back. "I didn't see Miranda that often, but I always looked forward to it. She was such a bright spirit. I can't imagine anyone wanting to kill her."

"I think the woman who killed her was in a very bad state emotionally and that discovering she'd been found out sent her over the edge. You could help to prove or disprove my theory. I would be very grateful to you."

"Usually this sort of request comes from the police," he said. His words were doubtful, but his eyes were sympathetic. "Why haven't you gone to them?"

"Because I'm a suspect myself," Claire admitted. "And I don't believe they'll listen to me. Would it be too much trouble to check and see if the x-rays are in the file? If they are here, I'm wrong and I'll forget about it."

"I'll look," Dr. Rule agreed.

Claire waited impatiently while he was gone, staring at the clouds, listening to the tepid music. It was much harder than waiting to discover if she needed a filling. The longer he was gone, the more her doubt expanded until it became a balloon filling the room and pressing against her chest.

When Dr. Rule returned he held an empty black plastic frame. The light shining through the holes reminded Claire of light coming through a cow vertebra in a Georgia O'Keeffe painting. Dr. Rule showed her that the name written on the black frame was Miranda Kohl.

"I'm sorry it took so long," he said. "I had to calm an anxious child on my way back. I'm afraid you are right about the x-rays. This mount should be full."

It was what Claire had expected, but seeing the emptiness in the mount didn't make her feel any better. "How could someone steal x-rays from your office?" she asked.

Dr. Rule gave her an embarrassed smile. "It wouldn't be that hard. New River is still a small town. We don't expect people to come in here and steal x-rays. We leave the door unlocked when we go to lunch so if our one-o'clock appointments arrive early our patients don't have to wait outside."

"Do you have another set anywhere?"

"No."

"How long would it take for you to notice the x-rays were gone?"

"We might never notice if Miranda didn't come back, unless we got a request from another dentist or the police."

"Could you tell by looking at the corpse's mouth whether or not she was Miranda even without the x-rays?"

258

"I believe I could. Miranda was an actress and you know how they are about teeth in Hollywood. She took excellent care of hers. Her fillings were all porcelain inlays. She didn't have a single silver amalgam filling. She did have one rather sloppy crown that another dentist put in."

"Do you have a record of who that dentist is?"

"I'm afraid I don't. Would you like me to get in touch with the police?"

"I don't know what to do. I probably should discuss it with my lawyer."

"I'd feel awful if that body were Miranda's."

"Do you know her husband, Erwin?"

"Yes, but not well. I see him occasionally at social functions. I'd like to think that if his wife was missing he'd go looking for her, but maybe not. It's rumored that he's in it for the money and he plays around when she's gone."

It was Claire's nature to be honest but reserved. Dr. Rule's understanding manner overcame her reserve and tapped into her honesty. "I didn't know Miranda that well," she admitted. "But I hate to think of her being married to a man who played around and used her money. He's been telling people in town that she left him."

"It's possible. The house has been rather quietly on the market. It's not listed with brokers, but a doctor friend of mine looked at it." His expression turned serious. "Do you think Erwin might have had something to do with her death?"

"Yes, but I don't know what," Claire replied.

"You will let me know what happens, won't you?" The possibility of playing detective appeared to intrigue him.

"Yes," Claire said. "I'm hoping that the Santa Fe police will contact you, but in the meantime it would be better if you didn't mention this to anyone. I don't want Erwin to know that I have suspicions."

Dr. Rule put his finger to his mouth. "My lips are sealed," he said.

Claire left his office feeling that she had an ally, at least for a while. She suspected that if he didn't hear from her soon Dr. Rule would go to the Santa Fe police, which might not be a bad thing, depending on the timing. Life was often a matter of timing. Claire was curious about the manner in which Jerry Bartlett lived. She didn't know whether the timing was right to drive by Jerry Bartlett's residence — it was morning and she could easily be spotted — but unless she stayed another night, daylight was the only time she had. She followed her computer map to the Bartlett residence and found a trailer surrounded by a corral. It was a beautiful setting and the corral had several horses in it, but it was still a trailer. The contrast between this residence and Miranda's was extreme. It wasn't hard to imagine that Jerry might want to move from the trailer to the big house and see Erwin as the means to do it.

Dr. Rule had been a comforting presence. If Claire had really had a toothache, she knew she would have left his office feeling that problem was solved, but as it stood, the disturbance in her soul had intensified. She saw the long drive home as an opportunity to work out her feelings and looked forward to it. Before she left New River, however, she decided to go by Miranda's house to see if there were any more secrets to be revealed.

Chapter Eighteen

She worked through the possibilities as she drove to Miranda's. Whoever had stolen her x-rays must have inserted them in Evelyn's mount in her dentist's office. The dentist passed them on to the police without noticing they were the wrong x-rays. Evelyn was a new patient and the dentist didn't know her well, or maybe he didn't take the time to know her well because she wasn't successful or interesting or attractive. If Miranda was dead, then Evelyn was likely to be alive. It would have been far easier for her to have switched the x-rays than it would have been for anyone else. Patients were often left alone with their records in a dentist's office. If Evelyn had killed Miranda, it would have only taken a day to steal the x-rays from Dr. Rule and another day to place them in her own dentist's office. She could have gotten an appointment with her dentist the same way Claire did with Dr. Rule, by feigning a toothache. Considering Evelyn's isolation she could easily have assumed it would be some time before the body in her house was discovered.

Claire thought about the body on the

floor, the bleached hair and the turquoise dress, which would have looked terrible on the plain Evelyn. Miranda's hair color changed frequently. It might have been blond on the day she went to Evelyn's house. Claire tried to replay the scene in her mind and put all the pieces together. The argument began outside. The runner went by, saw them and heard Evelyn call Miranda a bitch. They went into the house and ended up in the kitchen. Evelyn blew up in anger and hit Miranda with the frying pan. Prints on the frying pan matched those of the victim. Either Miranda tried to defend herself, or Evelyn put the prints there after Miranda was dead. The prints on Amaral's *Confidence-Man* also matched those on the victim, which would indicate that the book had once belonged to Miranda. Evelyn wouldn't want to linger in the house with a dead body so she tossed the frying pan and towel in a garbage bag, grabbed what was handy, including Miranda's ID, and fled in Miranda's vehicle. She threw the garbage bag out the window on her way south on I-25. Somewhere on the road she came up with the plan to switch the x-rays. Claire hoped that Evelyn hadn't sold her *Confidence-Man* before the encounter with Miranda. That

Evelyn had recognized the value of the book and taken it with her as something portable and saleable. That one day, when she needed the money or thought enough time had elapsed that she wouldn't be caught, she would try to sell it. It was one way Claire could think of to catch her.

She drove down the narrow driveway just beyond the reach of the cactus, parked her truck, got out and stood in front of Miranda's silent house. Noticing that the day had turned cloudy and the wind had picked up, she took her windbreaker from the cab and put it on, feeling the weight of the tape recorder she'd left in the pocket. The only change she saw here was that Jerry's horse had left droppings in the driveway. Claire followed the path around the house. As she peered in the windows, she saw that the half-full bottle of Corona was still on the kitchen counter next to the phone and a notepad, and the Topsiders and khakis remained on the floor in the bedroom. There was no sign that either Erwin or Miranda had returned. Jerry apparently hadn't taken it upon herself to enter the house and clean it up. When Claire reached the library window, she lingered, staring at the books on the shelves, wishing she could get close enough to discern the titles and the quality of the bindings. The books might be decoration, but her impression was that someone in this house loved books. There were more books in this library than there were in her bedroom. In her case she had read most of them. Erwin was now the most likely suspect to have put *The Confidence-Man* in her office. If he had, his fingerprints could be on it. Claire wondered whether she or Sid Hyland could persuade Amaral to check the book for Erwin's fingerprints. He might consider this turn of events far-fetched. She hoped Dr. Rule would remain an ally. Without the x-rays it would only be his word that the body was Miranda's, but if he could describe her teeth accurately and in detail his word would be convincing. A DNA test would establish definitively whether or not the body was Miranda's — if Amaral could be persuaded to do one. He hadn't gone to the trouble and expense earlier when the dental evidence indicated the corpse was Evelyn Martin.

Claire stared at the tinted bronze glass in the window, shifting her focus back and forth between the books on the shelf and her own reflection, wondering what part Erwin had played in all of this. Had he planned a murder or merely taken advantage of it? How had he convinced Amaral that

Miranda was on location if she was really dead? Fraudulent documents? Impersonation? He had an actor's skills, but he'd struck a false note by pretending to be Miranda in the e-mails. The language used was his, not Miranda's. Claire hadn't remembered Miranda expressing anger to Elizabeth, and Lynn had confirmed that memory. She wondered how long Erwin could keep up the pretense of Miranda being alive. Long enough to sell the house and take the money to Mexico? If he had joint ownership, he might find a way to forge Miranda's name on the documents and transfer the title without her.

Claire stood at the window shifting her focus and feeling the wind at her back. Somewhere between her own reflection and the books on the shelf, she detected motion in the glass. Either a cactus had taken a step forward or someone was behind her. She spun around and saw Erwin Bush. Jerry must have told him she'd been here.

"What are you doing?" he asked.

"I'm looking for Miranda," Claire replied.

"Didn't I tell you she was in Mexico?" He came a step closer, leading with his taut drum of a stomach. Claire was reminded that he wasn't any taller than she was, but he was broader and quite possibly stronger. No doubt he was more cunning, but was he more ruthless? The moment was approaching when she could have the chance to find out. The fact that this meeting was taking place on Erwin's turf worked to his advantage. But it was also taking place in the desert, which could work to Claire's advantage. She knew the desert and never made the mistake of thinking that it was a benevolent place. She had a heightened sense of awareness and danger here. Her adrenaline level was rising and she hoped she'd have enough of it to stand her ground. She saw power in facing Erwin, capitulation and weakness in walking away.

"You did tell me Miranda was in Mexico," Claire replied, trying to keep her voice level and calm. "I was visiting Lynn and Steve. I thought possibly she'd be home by now and if so, it would be good to visit with her."

"She told me you'd been e-mailing each other," Erwin said.

"We have," Claire replied. She turned toward the building. "You have a beautiful house."

"We like it."

Claire glanced through the window. "I've been admiring your book collection. Did you know that I'm a librarian and my job involves buying rare books for the Center for Southwest Research at UNM?"

"Really?"

"Yes," Claire said, gauging his reaction to see how good a liar he was; she was convinced that by now he knew exactly where she worked. She had the impression that he was reaching into a pocket, pulling out an expression of surprise and pasting it on. It was an expression that was exaggerated enough to reach the back row.

"Miranda is responsible for this room and all the other rooms in the house," he said. "She's into Feng Shui and has exquisite taste, but to be honest, she chose those books for the color of the bindings, not the content. Miranda is not a reader."

"Are you?" Claire asked.

"I like to read," Erwin admitted. "I'm alone a lot when Miranda is on the road. Would you like to see the library up close?" He took a set of keys from his pocket and jangled them in his hand.

Under ordinary circumstances Claire would have loved to have seen the library, but the circumstances were not exactly ordinary. If Erwin intended to harm her, he could do so inside or out. Both were isolated, but there were ways she felt safer outside; the setting was more familiar and the escape route clear. The resident raven flapped its wings and flew away. She was reminded that yesterday she had told Lynn and Steve she was leaving for New Mexico, and she had told the center she wouldn't be back until tomorrow. If she didn't come back, it would be some time before anyone missed her. But Erwin needn't know that. It was hard to pass up a chance to see a beautiful library, particularly this beautiful library where she might find evidence that would clear her name. She looked through the glass, memorizing where the relevant objects were.

"All right," she said.

She followed Erwin around the house and across the patio to the kitchen door, where he inserted one of his keys in the lock. All the other keys on the chain jangled as he unlocked the door. The raven cawed again as if warning "don't go," but Claire straightened her back and entered the house.

Erwin stopped at the kitchen counter and asked if she wanted something to drink.

"No," she said.

"Mind if I have one?"

"Go ahead."

While he took a Corona from the refrigerator, Claire glanced at the notepad on the counter and saw that it was a shopping list. Erwin popped the cap and took a loud sip, playing the part of an uncouth beer guzzler. He was a man who played many parts. Claire wondered which was the real Erwin Bush — if there was a real Erwin Bush. He put the bottle down and began walking through the large house. She followed him across tiled floors, polished wood floors, Navajo rugs and Oriental rugs as he led her to the library. The floor in this room had a thick, white Berber carpet that swallowed the sound of footsteps. The room seemed wrapped in a cocoon of silence the way a library ought to be.

"May I look at the books?" Claire asked Erwin.

"Of course," he said, "be my guest." He stood still in the middle of the room and folded one arm across the other.

Claire walked up to the books looking for some organization to the shelving. Many of the books were bound in leather. She saw patches of deep red bindings complimented by forest green bindings; rusty orange balanced by navy blue in an arrangement as artful as a painting. The color she sought in the mix was warm brown. When she found it, she went to that section and placed her hand on the spine of the first book she came to.

"May I?" she asked. "It's always a pleasure to examine a fine book."

"Of course," Erwin replied again. He remained standing in the middle of the room but began shifting his weight from one foot to the other and rattling the keys in his pocket.

Claire knew that books should be shelved tight enough to support each other and stay erect — a tilted book became a warped book. But the books shouldn't be so tight that they were pressed together. There was wiggle room on this shelf and the book she had chosen, Herman Melville's first novel, *Typee*, slipped easily from its place. She cradled it in her hands, wishing she wore gloves and detecting a slightly musty smell, which wouldn't have come from this house but could have come from a previous owner. She turned to the copyright page and saw that, as she had expected, this was a first edition. Next she went to the title page and saw that it wasn't a signed first edition. These weren't books a decorator selected merely because they looked good on the shelf. This was a complete set of rare first editions that had been rebound in full morocco. As she put *Typee* back Claire noticed that *Omoo*, the adjacent book, had tilted into the empty space. She straightened it

271

then walked past the remaining Melvilles, finding them in order, except that *The Piazza Tales* abutted the book that was published posthumously, *Billy Budd, Sailor*. She continued examining the shelves until she had worked her way to the far side and stood adjacent to the fireplace.

She turned toward Erwin, whose expression had become watchful and alert, one expression that didn't appear to be a performance. He had stopped shifting from one foot to the other. His weight was evenly balanced, his knees were slightly bent, the hand holding the keys was still.

Claire's right hand was at her side. Her left hand slipped into the pocket of the windbreaker, where it landed on the tape recorder. She felt for the record button and pushed it while she said, "Your copy of *The Confidence-Man* is missing."

It was the moment to see who was the better performer, the person with experience or the novice. His role was to feign ignorance. Hers to feign confidence. Erwin laughed and took a step closer. "Are you sure?"

"Yes."

"It must be on the shelves somewhere, misshelved by Miranda or the maid. Miranda was always rearranging the books.

272

She paid more attention to color than to author or title."

Claire's right hand reached behind her back. "Actually it was misshelved in my office. Detective Amaral found it there concealed beneath the dust jacket of *The Scarlet Letter.*"

His attempt to mold his face into an expression of surprise convinced her that he was a bad actor. "Why would the detective look in your office?"

"Someone told him that was where the book would be, someone who is trying to frame me. I'm the only known victim of Evelyn Martin who doesn't have an alibi for the night she was presumed murdered. Finding the book in my office made it appear that I was in Evelyn Martin's house that night. That I killed her, took it back and concealed it in my office."

Erwin rearranged his rubbery features into an expression of false puzzlement. "Are you suggesting that Miranda is trying to frame you?"

"No. I'm saying that you are."

Erwin sprung forward, moving surprisingly quickly for a heavy man. It only took a few leaps for him to cross the room, invade Claire's space and make her feel threatened. "Why would I want to do that?" he asked.

Claire grabbed the handle of the object behind her and yanked it from the rack. It was an elegant brass-handled poker that resembled a rapier. Up close it was pointed and vicious. She jabbed the poker at Erwin with the sensation that his taut belly would puncture and deflate once the weapon made contact. Actually it felt firm and unyielding until Erwin groaned and stepped backward, clutching a bloody stain on his shirt.

"You stabbed me," he said.

"You attacked me."

"I didn't attack you. You just surprised me with that accusation. That's all." He stared at the wound, but it appeared to be a surface scratch that wouldn't deter him.

"I told the Grangers I was coming here," Claire lied. "They'll be alarmed if I don't get back soon." Not being sure whether Erwin believed her or not, she kept the poker aimed at him. "Miranda's dead, isn't she?" she asked.

"Dead?" he asked, pretending disbelief but doing it rather badly, Claire thought.

"Dead," she repeated. "You can stop performing now, Erwin. I know Miranda is dead, and I know how to prove it." Although she spoke these words with more conviction than she felt, Erwin seemed to believe her.

He sighed and stepped back, appearing relieved to give up the pretense.

"If she is," he said, "I didn't kill her. Evelyn Martin did. Once Lynn told Miranda she'd been robbed by Evelyn, it confirmed her suspicion that Evelyn had framed her all those years ago. She had to be at a presentation in Santa Fe. She wanted to have it out with Evelyn and she looked her up."

"How did she know that Evelyn lived in Santa Fe?"

"Where do middle-aged women in the Southwest go when they're looking for a new life? Santa Fe. Miranda searched the white pages on the Internet and found Evelyn's address."

"What color was Miranda's hair then?"

"Blonde. When she went to Santa Fe, I went to Mexico. Miranda and I were estranged and spending very little time together. She intended to file for divorce. Marriages between actors are a struggle. One's career goes up, the other's goes down. It makes for competition and tension. Three weeks after Miranda went to Santa Fe, I came back home and found she wasn't here. Steve told me about Evelyn's death, how the body had been too decomposed to recognize, about the turquoise dress Evelyn was wearing. Miranda owned a turquoise dress."

In Claire's opinion, to have told no one about Miranda's disappearance went beyond coldhearted and opportunistic into criminal territory. "How could you not tell anyone?" she asked. "You believed your wife was dead. Why didn't you call the police?"

Erwin shuffled his feet as he attempted to justify his behavior. "I was embarrassed we were so estranged that I didn't notice her absence for weeks. I didn't wish her dead, but there were ways I could benefit from it. Miranda had written me out of her will, leaving everything to charity and distant relatives. She intended to put the house in her name only. I was looking for a place in Mexico. If I kept quiet, I thought I could sell this house and get myself some money for a new start. Whenever anyone called, I told them Miranda was on location in Mexico. If they had to be in touch with her, I e-mailed them under her name. I faked an affidavit from a producer for Amaral. I had a friend call him and claim to be Miranda."

"Jerry Bartlett?"

"Yeah," Erwin admitted, showing no regret about implicating a friend.

"Did you ever intend to tell anyone?" Claire asked him.

"Of course," was Erwin's blustery response. "As soon as I was settled in Mexico, I intended to tell the detective the truth and help him find Miranda's killer."

Claire doubted that, imagining that once the house was sold and the money in his pocket, Erwin Bush would disappear and the man standing in front of her now would turn into someone else. Someone with a different name and a different persona, although it would be hard to change his physical appearance.

"You don't believe me, do you?" he asked, taking a step closer.

Claire straight-armed the poker and said, "No."

Erwin stood still, crossing one arm over the other. "Did I really do anything criminal when you stop and think about it?"

"You lied," she said. "You concealed a death, you forged a document, you planted evidence in my office."

"Would that be enough to drag me out of Mexico for? I believe that once Amaral learns Evelyn killed Miranda he'll forget all about me. I'm not a murderer, only a petty criminal, an out-of-work actor trying to find a way to survive. You can put the poker down now."

Claire ignored him, tightening her grip on

the handle. "I'm taking a book with me."

"Whatever," Erwin said. "Are we done?" He touched the bloody spot on his shirt.

"Almost," Claire said. She went to the Melville section, took off her windbreaker, wrapped it around *The Piazza Tales* and lifted it from the shelf. Still holding the poker in her right hand she headed for the door.

"Shall I walk you to your car?" Erwin asked.

"No."

"One more thing," he said. "You might tell your detective that someone has been using Miranda's credit cards in Los Angeles. The bills have been coming here."

Claire left Erwin standing in the middle of the library and found her way down the hallway, listening for the sound of his footsteps behind her but hearing nothing. Now that she was certain Miranda was dead, the paintings, the rugs, the furniture, the beautiful objects seemed to be whispering, "Who will take care of us now that she is gone?" She hoped they would end up with someone who appreciated them. As she passed through the kitchen she grabbed the notepad beside the phone and put that in her pocket, too. When she reached the front door, she let herself out. She was still clutching the poker when she got to her truck, but once the engine was running, she dropped it onto the gravel and left it there, thinking this house was where it belonged. Her relief at solving the crime and clearing her own name was tempered by a sadness that this house would never again be home to Miranda.

She suspected that Erwin would pack up the most valuable objects and that it wouldn't be long before he followed her down the road with a loaded SUV.

Chapter Nineteen

She stopped at the Fina station, called Sid Hyland from the pay phone and told him all she had learned in New River. He managed to listen without interruption.

"Let me get this straight," he said once she had finished. "You're telling me you believe the body found in the Santa Fe house is Miranda Kohl and not Evelyn Martin?"

"Yes. I have a tape of Erwin Bush, Miranda's husband, saying that he thinks so, too. The Santa Fe Police Department used fraudulent dental records when they identified the body as Evelyn Martin, and Miranda Kohl's dentist here can prove that."

"Are you coming back to Albuquerque now?"

"I plan to."

"Call my office in the morning and make an appointment. I'd like to see you tomorrow."

"I'm afraid Erwin is going to get in his vehicle and head for Mexico. Is there any way to keep him in the country until this is sorted out? Could the local police hold him?"

"Based on what you've told me, no. Has he harmed you physically? Do you feel you are in any danger? Did he follow you?"

Claire looked down the highway and didn't see any vehicles that bore a resemblance to Erwin's SUV. "No," she said.

"I think you should get in your car and come back to Albuquerque. We'll talk tomorrow."

She suspected that by the time she reached Flagstaff Erwin would be on his way to Mexico. Nevertheless she kept her eye on the rearview mirror as she climbed I-17. Every time she saw a black SUV coming up behind her, she slowed down and let it go by. When she got to Flagstaff she turned east on I-40. Now she had to worry about the sun setting in her rearview mirror and keeping all the semis on the road from blocking her way or boxing her in. Sometimes she looked in her rearview mirror and saw one barreling down on her, painted, polished and decorated with the loving care of a low-rider.

She had hoped to be home by dark, but by the time she reached Grants night had fallen. There were no more slick paint jobs to study once the sun set, only the arrangement and intensity of lights. Red lights and white lights outlined the shapes of tractor trailers in the dark. The road wasn't any emptier at night. If anything, more long-distance truckers came out, but Claire's sense of solitude intensified and her thoughts changed. During daylight she had replayed the tape and was relieved that Erwin's statement came through loud and clear. After dark her thoughts turned to the woman who was dead and the one who was missing. She inserted a piano concerto into her tape deck in an attempt to restore order, but the tape jammed and she couldn't get it to play. She spun the radio dial but found nothing she wanted to listen to. She was left with the sound of the wind at her window and the wheels on the highway. One dark thought was that the light-as-a-butterfly Miranda had ended up a swollen corpse on Evelyn Martin's floor, and she would have to tell Lynn about it. For Lynn it would be more than the loss of a friend, it would be the end of a dream.

Claire's thoughts moved on to Evelyn. Now that she knew who had gone to the house, she saw the scene in the kitchen differently. Elizabeth and Ginny could well have lost control and threatened Evelyn, but she didn't see Miranda doing that. The murder might not have been an act of self-defense, but an attempt to prevent discovery. It made Evelyn's actions seem more cold and calculating. Up to the point when she wielded the frying pan, Evelyn had merely been a thief, Claire supposed, but now that she had become a murderer, what would that do to her state of mind? Had she used Miranda's credit cards in LA and, if so, was she still there? Claire saw it as a sprawling, anonymous place destructive to people with no roots or sense of identity, a place where people who were close to the edge fell off. What would she do when Miranda's credit ran out? Rob another friend? Evelyn never had many friends. Approaching other people from the U of A days would be risky since she had no way of knowing who had been informed that she was dead.

Claire was relieved to finally get off I-40 at Tramway and out of the path of the eighteen-wheelers. Nemesis waited for her at the door and she picked him up and gave him a long hug. She had been gone longer than she intended and his food dish was empty. She filled the dish, checked her phone messages and found one from Lynn saying she hoped Claire got home safely. She postponed calling her back and walked through her small, neat house, which would fit into one wing of Miranda's. It was comfortable but not elegant. She had some valuable things, some beautiful things, some that were neither. Many of them had been given her by family and friends. She treasured all of them, the plain as well as the beautiful. If there was Feng Shui in this house it had been created by love, not by money.

Ever since Evelyn robbed her, Claire had felt a disturbance in her home, but now she could see the possibility of restoring tranquility. She took the notepad, the tape recorder and the copy of *The Piazza Tales* wrapped in her windbreaker into her office and placed them on her desk.

Then she went to the guest room, took the black nightgown from the drawer, draped it in front of her and stood in front of the mirror thinking about identity and wondering how accurate an assessment Evelyn had made of her old friends when she'd chosen what to steal from them and what to give. Her visits to their houses gave her the opportunity to study what they owned and what that said about their characters. In Claire's experience the powerless always knew more about the powerful than the reverse. The servant studies the master, the master doesn't see the servant. Not that she and the other sisters had a lot of power, but Evelyn had so little. Claire had been busy with work during her visit and hadn't paid much attention to her. But Evelyn had been watching. What had she learned?

She'd taken a book from the shelf that had a high monetary value, but it wasn't one that Claire loved. The issue of the black nightgown was more complicated. Had Evelyn seen Claire as a woman who would ever wear (or want to wear) a silky black nightgown slit to the navel? Was Claire now or had she ever been that person? In her dreams, maybe. She remembered Evelyn at the sorority house saying, "*You* have cleavage." That was right before she went to Europe, met Pietro and spent a semester traveling around Europe and Morocco with him in a Volkswagen van that broke down in every country they visited. Claire wondered if Evelyn had seen a budding sensuality in her back then. Had she seen it again when she visited last spring? Or was it too late for sensuality to ever bloom again? Evelyn might have given her more of a gift than she'd intended.

While Claire stared at the mirror it turned into a window opening onto a street in Marrakesh. The trees were laden with oranges. The Atlas Mountains were tipped with snow. The sun was setting on one side, the full moon rising on the other. Soft voices on the street spoke in Arabic and French. A candle burned in the room. Behind her Pietro lay on the bed smoking hashish. Was she wearing black that night or nothing? Smoke filled the window and then it became a mirror again. Claire could see that the nightgown would fit, but how would she look in it at this point? Not willing to take the risk of finding out, she folded it up, wrapped it in tissue paper and put it back in the drawer.

She went to the living room, picked up the phone, called Lynn and broke the news that she believed Miranda had been murdered by Evelyn Martin.

"That can't be true," she protested. "It wasn't that long ago that I saw her."

"When was the last time you actually saw her?" Claire asked. "Not the last time you got an e-mail or saw the commercial on television but the last time you actually saw Miranda alive?"

"At Christmas, I guess," Lynn admitted. "I'll tell Steve to talk to Erwin. Erwin will tell him the truth."

"If Steve can find him."

"Let me check with Steve and I'll call you back," Lynn said.

When she called back two hours later, Claire was soaking in a tub of warm water lapping at the edges of sleep.

"There was no answer," Lynn said. "We drove over to New River and found no one home. I can't believe that Miranda is dead, Claire."

"It's hard to accept, I know, but it's the most logical explanation."

"It may be logical," Lynn said, "but to me it's horrible."

"I'm hoping to talk to Detective Amaral soon. If he can be persuaded to do a DNA test, he'll be able to establish for certain whether the body is Miranda's."

"You'll let me know what he says?"

"Immediately," Claire replied.

The next day she took the copy of *The Piazza Tales*, the notepad and the tape to Sid Hyland. Hyland was dubious about the value of any of them, pointing out to Claire that the book and notepad could have come from anywhere and the tape could be anyone's voice.

"Erwin is an actor," she said. "His voice should be on record somewhere if it gets down to that."

She persuaded Hyland to call Dr. Rule, and he came away from that call impressed by the dentist's ability to describe Miranda's teeth.

"He'd make a good witness," he said when he got off the phone. "He's knowledgeable, professional and precise. You need to talk to Amaral. Let me see if I can set up a meeting here."

Amaral agreed to come to Albuquerque two days later. Claire never wanted to see him in her office again; they would meet at Hyland's office at nine in the morning. She woke up early that day and prepared for the meeting by balancing militant tai chi exercises with calming tai chi. As she drove across town to Hyland's office, she wondered how Amaral would handle himself in front of a lawyer who was twenty years older and far more experienced.

Amaral got there first and both men were standing when she entered the room. The detective was as tall as Hyland, but Hyland outweighed him by fifty pounds. His manner was soft-spoken and deferential, as it had been to Claire when they first met, but by now Claire knew this was a mask that could be taken on and off at will. From the moment Claire entered the room Amaral avoided looking at her, averting his eyes like a guilty child. As requested, he had brought *The Confidence-Man* still concealed under the dust jacket of *The Scarlet Letter.*

Claire didn't waste any time playing Erwin Bush's tape. Amaral seemed startled, but dubious.

"How do I know that is Erwin Bush's voice?" he asked.

"He's an actor," Hyland replied. "His voice will be on record somewhere."

He'd quoted her rather well, Claire thought, except that he had said "will" where she had said "should."

"You won't need to compare voices once you have seen the rest of the evidence," Hyland added.

Claire put a wrapped copy of *The Piazza Tales* on Hyland's desk. "I took this book from Miranda Kohl and Erwin Bush's library," she said. "It was part of a complete set of Herman Melville. I believe *The Confidence-Man* you have is also a part of that set. It was the only book missing from the collection. The reason the fingerprints you found on your *Confidence-Man* match the body in Evelyn Martin's house is because the book is Miranda Kohl's and so is the body. If you will remove the jacket from your *Confidence-Man* I can demonstrate the similarities."

As the jacket came off, she had a moment of anxiety. Her goal was to convince a man who had shown no interest in rare books of the similarities between these two books. What if she had been wrong? The only way to be sure was to place them side by side for comparison. She put on her white gloves and unwrapped *The Piazza Tales*. The ostensible reason for wearing white gloves was to protect a rare book from fingerprints and damage, but putting them on also gave her an air of authority and of confidence.

Once the two books were together it was obvious that they were peas from the same pod. They were the same dimensions. The full brown morocco was identical in texture and in color. Both books had a similar amount of wear. Claire pointed out to Amaral and Hyland how the spines of the books had faded over time, but the fronts and backs had remained close to the original color. She demonstrated that the gilt letters on the spines and front covers were identical in style.

She opened them to the copyright pages and demonstrated that both books were first editions. *The Piazza Tales* had been published in 1856 and *The Confidence-Man* in 1857. The open books brought her to her next point. She took the notepad she had found in Miranda's house and placed it on the desk next to *The Confidence-Man*.

"Beer," the list read, "wine, milk, hamburger meat and cheese."

"That's a shopping list," Amaral said.

"It was written by Erwin Bush," Claire replied. "I found it in the house. It will be useful for comparing handwriting."

"Did your tip that *The Confidence-Man* was in Claire's office come from Erwin Bush?" Hyland asked.

"It was anonymous," Amaral replied.

Claire compared the handwriting. By now she knew the handwriting in Erwin's note well, but she had only seen the signature in *The Confidence-Man* briefly. She turned to the title page of *The Confidence-Man* and compared it to the note.

"Herman Melville died in 1891," she said. "As I said before this signature couldn't possibly be his. If it were, the ink would be faded and cracked. Even without an authentic Melville signature to compare it to, the ink told me that this was a forgery."

Amaral examined the signature. "I don't see any similarity between the two handwritings," he said.

This was where Claire felt on shakiest ground, wishing that the handwriting expert August Stevenson was here to help. The handwritings *were* different, but she attributed that to the deviousness of a single writer, not the differences between two.

"When people are trying to conceal their style of writing, they are likely to slant the script in a different direction," she said. "Notice how the Melville signature slants backward toward the left, not a natural way to write. Most people write in a hurry and slant forward toward the right. Another way people conceal their writing style is by squaring off the round letters and by adding or removing embellishments to the tall letters. But the inconsistency here is revealing. See how the *e*'s have been squared off in 'Herman Melville'? But the *a* is round, as it is in 'hamburger meat' in the note. The beginning letters in the signature — *H* and *M* — are large and bold with a dramatic flourish. That's the way a forger would expect the script of a well-known writer to appear. Yet the *l*'s in both documents have a plain and narrow loop."

Hyland nodded from the other side of the desk. They had discussed the possibility of her offering to be fingerprinted and she felt confident in taking the next step.

"I believe if you test both Melville books for fingerprints you won't find mine on either of them." She hoped Amaral wouldn't suggest at this point that she had worn white gloves every time she handled a piece of evidence. He may have been thinking it, but he didn't say it.

"I also believe you will find Erwin Bush's fingerprints on both *The Confidence-Man* and the notepad," Claire continued, "and that you may find Miranda Kohl's fingerprints in Evelyn Martin's house and possibly on the frying pan if she struggled to defend herself. There should be plenty of prints in Miranda's house for comparison." The best way to obtain Erwin Bush's fingerprints would be to find Erwin Bush, but Claire wasn't sure he would ever be found.

"Are you willing to consent to being fingerprinted now?" Amaral asked, facing her this time through the wire-rimmed glasses.

Claire was surprised that Sid Hyland's ego had let her do most of the talking so far. One reason for his success could be that he was capable of leaving expert testimony to the experts.

He spoke up now and said, "DNA testing will establish without a doubt whether the corpse is Miranda Kohl or Evelyn Martin."

"We don't do DNA testing when we have other means of identification," Amaral replied. "The corpse was identified as Evelyn Martin by dental records."

"Miranda Kohl's dentist in Arizona

claims that her x-rays were stolen from his office, and he is capable of describing her teeth in detail. You need to see if the x-rays used for identification match Dr. Rule's description. How well did your dentist know Evelyn Martin? How carefully did he look at the x-rays? Did he treat Evelyn Martin after the supposed time of death and provide her with an opportunity to substitute one x-ray for another? It is my belief that further examination of the dental records will give you ample justification for a DNA test." Sid Hyland had no compunction about telling Amaral how to do his job. In fact, he seemed to enjoy it.

He moved on to the credit cards. "Miranda Kohl's husband claims her credit cards have been used in Los Angeles."

"If we establish that the body on Tano Road was Miranda Kohl's, then I will investigate," Amaral said.

"Time is of the essence," Hyland reminded him. He was being overbearing, but Claire supposed that's what she was paying him for. She had no doubt that when his bill arrived it would be enormous, but if it removed her from suspicion it would be worth the cost.

Hyland looked at his watch, stood up and said, "I believe we are done here."

"I will need to take the notepad, the tape and the book as evidence," Amaral said.

Hyland handed them over. He and Claire had already made copies of the notepad and the tape.

"If you discover that Evelyn Martin is in Los Angeles, I may be able to help you find her," Claire said. It was her nature to be accommodating, but she also sensed that she had fallen into the role of playing good defendant to Hyland's bad lawyer.

"Thank you for your help," Amaral said, reverting to his previously deferential manner. He looked at her when he spoke, but his expression was difficult to read.

After he left the office, Claire asked Hyland what he thought.

"I believed from the very beginning that you would be your own best witness," he said. "I doubt if Evelyn Martin would do so well on her own behalf."

"She's a disturbed person," Claire agreed. Now that the attention had shifted from her to Evelyn, her concern was that Evelyn be apprehended. "Do you think she will ever be caught?"

"She might not," Hyland said. "She has shown some intelligence and the police in New Mexico aren't used to intelligent criminals. Credit card fraud is a federal crime, however. Help is available if Amaral is willing to ask for it."

Traffic was heavy on the drive back to CSWR, giving Claire time to mull over what he had said. Evelyn might have wondered if Claire had been Amaral's prime suspect but had no way of knowing for sure. If the Santa Fe police started looking for her, she wouldn't know that either unless they bungled the investigation. Claire would sleep better at night if Evelyn were caught, and she wondered if there was anything she could do to facilitate her capture. The best way to help would be to do what Evelyn had done — enter the mind of someone she had known many years ago. The thief studies the victim. The sleuth should study the thief. In her spare moments Claire tried to get inside Evelyn's mind. She'd crossed the line from thief to murderer. What would that do to her mental state? What would she do when the credit ran out? There might be other sorority sisters living in California, but contacting them would be a huge risk, a risk Claire wouldn't be willing to take if she were in Evelyn Martin's position.

Chapter Twenty

Claire believed that most legal jargon was boilerplate, but the phrase "time is of the essence" had a poetic ring. Time *was* of the essence, but it wasn't on her side when it came to apprehending Evelyn Martin. It would take time to get samples from Miranda's house that could be tested for DNA, time to compare them to samples taken from the body found on Tano Road. How long would Evelyn stay in California, if she was in California? People on the run tended to head west. If Evelyn got scared or ran out of credit, where would she go next? Hawaii?

Claire called Brett Moon in Los Angeles. "Have you heard anything about my *Confidence-Man*?" she asked him.

"Not a word," Brett said. "You may be sure that I'll call you the minute I do."

"I have reason to believe that the woman who took the book went to LA and used stolen credit cards there. Sooner or later her credit will run out, and I'm hoping she will try to sell the book. Could you put out word that you have a buyer for *The Confidence-Man* or would that be too obvious?"

"It would be obvious to me, but it might

not to a person who is desperate and doesn't know much about rare books."

"It might be better just to say you have a customer willing to pay a good price for a first-edition Melville, any Melville."

"If your thief is smart, she'll end up here anyway; this is where the book will bring the most money. I'll notify all the dealers in town that I have a customer, just in case."

"Thanks, Brett."

"Glad to help."

The phone became an instrument of torture. Claire waited for word from Brett or Hyland or Amaral, feeling all the while she was a silly schoolgirl hoping a potential boyfriend would call. The phrase "time is of the essence" played over and over in her mind like an annoyingly repetitive TV commercial.

It took a while for the call to come. When it finally did, she was at home trimming her rosebushes. As soon as she heard the phone ring, she dropped the branch she'd been trimming, pricking her finger on a thorn. "Damn," she swore. It was evening, the time when anonymous and unavailable were out trolling for suckers. No one she was expecting to call was likely to be working at this hour.

"You know better than to get excited about phone calls at this time of day," she said to herself as she ran to the house.

She picked up the phone hoping for news but saw "unavailable" appear on her caller I.D. She waited for the pause that comes before a computerized phone dialer kicks in.

"Claire." It was Sid Hyland speaking in his cowboy twang. "I have some damn good news. You are no longer a suspect in the death of Evelyn Martin. Her dentist examined his records more carefully and determined that the x-rays used to identify Evelyn Martin were not hers. Furthermore she showed up in his office on April twenty-third claiming she had a toothache. The dentist found nothing wrong and sent her on her way. The teeth in the corpse matched the description given by the dentist in Arizona. The police went to Miranda Kohl's home and did not find her or her husband. They did find hair in a comb and on her clothes that matched the hair found on your towel. It also matched the DNA in the corpse, but there was no match with any of Evelyn Martin's samples. Forensics determined that the corpse is Miranda Kohl. Either Evelyn Martin died somewhere else or —"

"Or she went to LA and used Miranda Kohl's credit cards," Claire finished his sentence for him.

"Entirely possible," Hyland said.

"What is being done to find her, do you know?"

"I don't," Hyland said. "I didn't see that as my concern now that you are no longer a suspect."

Claire wondered if he had already lost interest in the case and was ready to move on to the next one, or if he was thinking of how much he charged her every minute they talked. She was still very concerned with what had happened to Evelyn Martin.

"I have some ideas about how she might be found," she said. "Would you mind if I called Amaral and discussed them with him?"

"Just as long as you don't have anything criminal in mind." Hyland laughed at his own joke.

"I don't," Claire said. "Thank you very much for your help."

"My pleasure," he replied.

Apparently he didn't mind working late, but Detective Amaral had gone for the day when Claire called him. She left him a message to call back as soon as possible.

She knew she should call Lynn, but what

had been good news for her would be very upsetting to her friend. She thought about waiting until she was feeling less elated herself, but she kept her promise and called.

"Oh, God," Lynn said when she heard the body had been positively identified as Miranda. "I know you told me it was a possibility she was dead, but I kept hoping it wouldn't be true. Miranda was so talented and so full of life. Are you sure?"

"The police took DNA samples from her house in New River and compared them to the body. DNA evidence doesn't lie," Claire said.

"It's heartbreaking," Lynn replied. "And what makes it worse is that Evelyn will probably get away with it."

"Have you or Steve heard from Erwin?" Claire asked.

"Not a word."

Amaral called back in the morning before she left for work. She took the phone into her bedroom and sat down in the armchair surrounded by books. Books made good witnesses — silent, intelligent, dispassionate, calm.

"Ms. Reynier," he said. "Have you spoken to your attorney yet?" The tone of his voice had reverted to the polite, respectful, pearly manner it had when they first talked. Claire realized that she had been hearing disappointment in his voice in their more recent conversations, as if she had somehow let him down by becoming a murder suspect.

"Yes," Claire said. "He told me that DNA testing established that the body found on Tano Road is Miranda Kohl."

"We thank you for your help. I regret that the evidence seemed for a time to implicate you in the death of Evelyn Martin."

Claire understood that was as close as he would come to an apology and she accepted it. "I was wondering if there was any way I could help you further. I have some ideas about how you might be able to locate Evelyn Martin."

"Such as?" Amaral asked.

"Presumably you have been in touch with the credit card companies."

"Yes."

"Are Miranda Kohl's credit cards still being used in LA?"

"No. The credit ran out."

"I believe that if Evelyn had sold my *Confidence-Man* I would know it. It's a valuable book and when she runs out of friends to rob, she may well try to sell it. I think I know how to catch her if she does." She outlined her plan to Amaral.

He didn't object to the outline of her plan, although he wasn't enthusiastic about her participation. He insisted on communicating directly with Brett Moon.

Claire went back to waiting. She found any kind of waiting annoying, but long-distance, high-stakes waiting resembled a wire strung too tight that picked up every vibration. She continued to do her job while she waited to see what would happen in Los Angeles, but she was using only half her brain. The other half wandered around LA imagining what it would be like to be Evelyn Martin, wondering where her next dollar or scam would come from. The kind of loneliness and tension she was feeling had to be extreme.

Brett Moon agreed to call Detective Amaral the minute someone tried to sell him *The Confidence-Man* and he kept his word. Then he called Claire.

"I've notified the detective," he said, "but I also wanted to tell you that a woman went to Other World books in Venice with a *Confidence-Man* to sell and Thomas Barnes referred her to me. She called and I told her that I always have customers for a Melville first edition and made an appointment with her for tomorrow afternoon. This doesn't give the police much time, but I was afraid that if I postponed the meeting she would get away."

"Did she give you a name?"

"No. I asked, but she refused," he told her. "Your detective wanted to come but it's the LAPD's jurisdiction and they're going to send one of their own. I know their detective and I told him that your presence is absolutely totally necessary in order to identify the suspect and the book."

Claire knew that wasn't entirely true. The police had other ways of identifying the suspect and the book. But she appreciated Brett's efforts to include her.

"I said I wouldn't do it without you."

"Thanks," she said. "Did he agree?"

"Reluctantly," Brett said.

Claire knew Harrison would let her take the time off once she told him the purpose of the trip. Getting a flight to LA on such short notice was more difficult.

When she got to LAX she took a cab to Half Moon Books. On the ground LA was too many lanes of fast-moving traffic, but the store in Westwood Village was a serene place, a stone house that reminded her of an illustration in a children's book. A bell tinkled as Claire opened the door. Silence followed when she closed it, giving her the sense that she had stepped from the rush of the present to a stillness that was out of time. In her opinion the covers of books stopped time and held it in place. LA had a reputation for being a good book town, but it always surprised her that people who lived in a place so focused on the now would be interested in old books. Of course, there was liable to be more money in one square mile of Beverly Hills than there was in the entire state of New Mexico. People here loved entertainment and make-believe and could indulge in whatever whim they wanted to. It was well known that a book would bring more in LA or New York City than it would anywhere else. That's where a smart buyer would bring it to sell. Evelyn had proven that she had cunning if not a high level of intelligence. Claire didn't consider it intelligent to steal from one's friends, particularly when one had so few of them.

She stood still for a moment soaking up the ambiance of Half Moon Books. The carpet was thick and plush. The bookshelves had lattice doors that displayed the covers of the books but were locked tight. You can look, the doors said, but you mustn't touch. Illustrated books were open and on display in a glass case. The books in this room exuded value, but the really pricey books were in a back room locked tight in Brett Moon's safe.

No one came out to greet her. It appeared she was being left alone to browse, but she knew she was watched by a one-eyed camera mounted on the wall and that Brett himself, or one of his staff, was observing her every move and analyzing her potential as a buyer or a seller. If someone decided she was merely a browser, no one would come out. She might just be watched on the monitor until she gave up and went away. Claire wondered if that was how Evelyn Martin would have been treated, if she hadn't called first. Evelyn was a plain brown bird and in Los Angeles even book people tended to be macaws.

While she waited for someone in the back room to recognize her, Claire went to the glass case and admired the Maxfield Parrish illustrations in a Frank Baum book. There was no price beside the book, which meant she couldn't afford to buy it. Although she had plenty of books she could trade for it, if she ever became willing to part with one of her own books. She knew eventually Brett Moon would come out with his bald head glimmering like the full moon beneath the lights in the ceiling. His hand would be extended and he would say, "Claire. Ever so delighted to see you." But the fact that it was taking him so long to do so indicated someone somewhere considered her a browser and uninteresting. It was an assumption made about middle-aged women, an assumption it would please Claire to defy.

A bookshelf swung away from the wall and into the room and Brett swept out from behind it dressed in khakis and a white shirt but wrapped in an atmosphere of black-velvet intrigue and red-satin drama. He extended his hand and spoke the very words Claire had expected with the exact inflection she had expected.

"Claire. Ever so delighted to see you."

She took the cool white hand. "Hello, Brett," she said. "Nice to see you, too."

"I trust you had a good trip."

"I did."

He looked at his watch. "You're early."

"I'm always early. It's a character flaw."

"Being early can be a feat in LA traffic. Would you like to go out for coffee while we're waiting for the detective to show up?"

"If you don't mind, I'd just like to wait in the back room. I wouldn't want Evelyn to see me somewhere and get scared off."

"Of course," Brett said.

He led her through the bookcase-door into his study, which was the MGM version of a library. Miranda Kohl's decorator was outclassed in this room. The fine Oriental carpet on the floor was gently worn, as was the brown leather sofa and armchairs. The walls were covered with books, but books that were chosen for their content and their condition, not the color of their bindings, although some of the bindings happened to be magnificent.

Brett sat down behind his desk and clicked the bookcase-door shut with a remote control. Claire sat on the sofa. His eyes had a greedy gleam as he asked, "What do you plan to do with your *Confidence-Man* once we get it back? I have a buyer if you choose to sell."

"Harrison Hough?"

"He has expressed an interest, but now that this book has a story the town will be full of buyers. The LAPD Art Fraud Unit has assigned Detective Jorge Serafin to the case. Jorge has investigated thefts from some of the biggest names in the business. Any stolen object that he recovers automatically goes up in value. There is a movie in development right now about Jorge. Harrison Hough can't afford your book anymore."

"The LAPD has an Art Fraud Unit?" Claire asked.

"They do. Technically, books aren't art fraud, but they're close enough for the LAPD. I'll be happy to take the book on consignment for you."

"Actually, Brett, I'm planning to put it back on my shelf."

"It doesn't hold bad vibrations that will disturb the harmony of your collection?"

"A few," Claire admitted.

The bell that tinkled in the outer room clanged in the inner room. Brett looked at his monitor and said, "Jorge." He clicked the remote and the bookshelf swung open. "Come on in," he called.

The detective knew the drill and walked into the back room. He was tall, slender, silver haired and wore a well-fitted suit. If she hadn't known better, Claire would have pegged him as an actor rather than a detective. He'd be capable of playing himself in the movie, if the story of Jorge Serafin ever became a movie.

Brett introduced him to Claire and they exchanged pleasantries. They sat down on the leather furniture and Serafin queried Claire about what to expect from Evelyn Martin.

"She's a depressed person. I wouldn't

have thought her capable of murder, but it's possible her depression comes from repressed anger. Evelyn envied her old friends who had done something with their lives. The anger might have burst out of her when she was found out by Miranda Kohl. It was either that or the fear of discovery."

"What can you tell me about her body language?" Detective Serafin asked.

An actor's question, Claire thought. "When I last saw her she had the posture of a depressed person. Her shoulders were hunched. Her spine seemed compressed." Claire considered whether Serafin had noticed her own straight-backed posture and suspected that he had.

"Tell me about her hair."

"It was bleached."

"And her teeth?"

"They're dingy," Claire said.

"Does she have any distinguishing facial characteristics or expressions?" he asked.

"She has the stiff upper lip of a person who has been hurt or has had a collagen implant."

While they talked Claire watched the monitor for some sign of the person she had described. As the hour set for the meeting approached, Brett went to the front room and sat at the counter pretending to be studying a price guide while the ceiling light beamed down on his bald head. The detective and Claire fell silent. The seller was late and Claire became anxious she wouldn't show up at all. Finally the doorbell tinkled gently in the outer room and sounded an alarm in the inner room. Serafin went into alert mode, got off the sofa and stood behind Claire at the monitor. The door to Half Moon Books opened and a woman entered.

"Is that her?" Serafin asked.

"I don't know," Claire admitted. The face on the monitor filled her with a sickening sense of doubt. This was not the woman she had just described to the detective. This woman's blond hair was worn in an expensive layered cut. Her face was professionally made-up and her chin was firm. She carried herself well and wore the type of fitted black pantsuit favored by professional women, a suit designed to make a woman look thinner, but even so this woman had to be twenty pounds lighter than Evelyn Martin was the last time Claire saw her. How long had that been? Claire wondered. Almost a year and a half. Could Evelyn have lost that much weight in that amount of time? The front room was not wired for sound so they couldn't hear what the woman and Brett Moon said.

"She looks like a TV actress," Detective Serafin said, wrapping the word *TV* in the quotation marks of disdain.

Could there possibly have been an error in the DNA test? Claire wondered. In the samples given or in the process itself? Was there a layer of fraud that she hadn't discovered yet? The woman in the outer room smiled at Brett with expensive white teeth. Claire felt as if a trap door had opened beneath her and she was tumbling through a vacuum. "I don't recognize her," she said from her downward spiral.

The woman had a shopping bag. As she reached into it, Serafin's hand moved toward the weapon concealed beneath his suit jacket. He exhaled when the hand came out holding a book. Claire exhaled herself when she saw that the book had the cover of her *Confidence-Man*.

"Is that your book?" Amaral asked.

"I believe it is."

Claire wished it had been possible for Brett to wear white gloves when he handled the book, but it would have made him look very suspicious. He held it in his bare hands and examined it with agonizing slowness. He turned to the copyright page. He turned to the title page. He took out a magnifying glass and examined the signature. He looked at the woman, appearing to make her an offer. The woman hesitated. Claire knew Brett well enough that he wouldn't offer anyone a penny more than a book was worth. He spoke again. They agreed and shook hands. Brett's knee pushed a button beneath the counter and the bookshelf-door swung open. The detective drew his weapon and pounced through the opening.

"What is this?" The woman turned and her lips twisted in anger.

Claire followed the detective through the door and faced the woman still full of doubt. How could the elegant person in the sleek black pantsuit be the drab Evelyn Martin?

It might have been smarter for her to have pretended she didn't know Claire, but she was so stunned by her appearance that she said, "Well, look at *you*." Her upper lip was stiff but full of fissures, and the red lipstick bled into the cracks.

"Hello, Evelyn," Claire said. It was the moment of vindication. Evelyn had stolen valuable objects from her former friends. She had murdered Miranda Kohl and used stolen money to alter her appearance. She deserved whatever punishment she got. Yet as she watched the woman's chin droop and her posture sag while she reverted from the part of a woman full of confidence to the reality of the desperate Evelyn Martin, Claire felt no sense of triumph.

Chapter Twenty-one

She flew back to Albuquerque that evening. After she got to work in the morning she went to Harrison's office and found him sitting at his desk with the papier-mâché folk art figure of death pulling a cart across the shelf behind him. Harrison rarely showed reverence for anything, but he was in awe when he heard the signed first edition of *The Confidence-Man* had been recovered and would be returned to Claire as soon as it was no longer needed as evidence.

"This is one signed first edition of Herman Melville's that I don't have," he said in the hushed tone he reserved for dead white male writers. That they were the only writers worth studying was a view that had finally fallen out of favor elsewhere, but not in Harrison Hough's office.

"I'm aware of that," Claire said.

"Tell me the story of how the book was recovered."

She told him about Evelyn Martin's arrest, adding, "Brett Moon says the value of anything recovered by Detective Serafin goes way up in Los Angeles."

"You didn't make an agreement with

Brett Moon, did you, after I told you how interested *I* was?"

"I haven't made an agreement with anyone," Claire replied.

Harrison's fingers tapped the desk. "How much would you like for it?" he asked.

Claire had the impression he'd be willing to raid his children's college fund and refinance his house if necessary. "It's not for sale," she said.

"I beg your pardon."

"I said the book is not for sale. If you want to complete your Melville collection, you will have to find a signed first edition somewhere else."

He glared at her. She stared back thinking how unprofessional and inappropriate it was for Harrison to try to pressure her into selling him the book. The evidence she had of his plagiarism gave her confidence. She didn't want to get involved in the turmoil that revealing it would bring, but the fact that she knew about it and could prove it gave her a determination he might not have seen in her before. She raised her chin and straightened her back, signaling she was ready to go to the edge if need be.

Taking subservience for granted, Harrison didn't notice her determination. "How much would you like?" he asked again.

"The book is not for sale." She paused for emphasis between her words as if she were establishing authority over a naughty child.

Harrison's hand dropped into his lap. The room became silent while he took her measure. She hoped he would see that her determination was absolute and that she had something to back it up. He had expected her to be a pushover. He might even have thought he would get the book cheap, but now she saw doubt drifting across his eyes.

"It's not for sale, Harrison," she said again, somewhat more gently than she had the last time, but still holding firm.

"You're certain?"

"Yes."

"Your choice, of course." He waved his hand in a dismissive gesture. She walked back to her office, wondering if he was contemplating any retaliatory action, knowing she held the trump card if he did.

She wanted to tell John Harlan about her Los Angeles adventure, expecting he would share her joy in the recovery of the book, her ambivalence about the capture of Evelyn Martin and her small but significant triumph over Harrison. She intended to ask him if he'd have dinner with her, but she had a day full of meetings and appointments and didn't have time to call. On her way home from work, she stopped at Page One, Too. John always worked late and she expected him to be at the store. The parking lot in this mall was a complicated maze, full of signs saying "ONE WAY — DON'T ENTER" in all the places she wanted to enter. She negotiated her way through the lot, dodging vehicles backing out of parking spaces as well as vehicles that hadn't followed the DON'T ENTER signs. Usually she had to park at the far end of the mall and walk, but this evening she found a space near the door to Page One, Too. She pulled into it and turned off the ignition.

As she put her hand on the door handle to let herself out of the truck, she glanced toward the store and saw John coming out the front door. He wasn't alone. In fact, he was with the auburn-haired woman she had seen before in his office. John laughed and the woman laughed back. Claire looked down quickly, pretending to be searching for something in her purse, hoping they wouldn't walk by the truck and notice her. She waited for a knock on the window or a "Hey, Claire," but none came. When she looked up again John and the woman were getting into his car.

She waited until they had left the parking lot, then started her truck and drove home wondering exactly how involved John was with this woman. She would miss his conversation and companionship if he became involved with someone else. She should be happy for him if he had found someone who would offer him the warmth that she hadn't. It wasn't happiness she felt as she drove home but it wasn't deep regret either.

When she got to her house, she went to her bedroom and stood before the shelf where *The Confidence-Man* belonged, pleased that the book would be returned and order would be restored. It had had an adventure and gained a backstory. Claire often thought that when she wasn't watching, the characters in her books stepped out of their bindings and wandered. Sometimes she imagined she heard them gossiping, flattering or arguing as they communicated with each other. Every character in these books was another person's mind creature that had become her own. She thought about the power of imagination and how creativity required going into the depths to reach the heights. The trick was to go far enough to have an authentic experience, but not so far that it was impossible to find one's way back. The phrase "into the darkness looking for light" came to mind.

Wondering if there was light in the darkness she had just experienced, she took the Oxford World's Classics edition from her office to her spare bedroom. She opened the drawer containing the black nightgown and laid the book beside it. She would consider this her dark drawer, her Pandora's box, the place where the symbols of human weakness, maliciousness, avariciousness and destructiveness would be kept in the dark, shut off, but accessible to her when she felt the need to be reminded. She thought about putting on the black nightgown, then decided it wasn't necessary. Wearing the nightgown and seeing herself as she looked now might divert her from her purpose. Claire closed the drawer with the sense of finality that comes from finishing a chapter in a book. All she had learned from the chapter would stay with her, but it was time to begin another.

Wrapped in a layer of anticipation over a layer of trepidation, she went to her office, sat down at her desk and turned on her computer. She clicked on the search engine and typed in the name of Pietro Antonelli.